# SMOKY MOUNTAIN MYSTERIES

### Stories About
### Magnificent Mountains
### Unique People

# Juanitta Baldwin

# SMOKY MOUNTAIN MYSTERIES

### Stories About
### Magnificent Mountains
### Unique People

## Juanitta Baldwin

Suntop Press
A Division of Suntop, Inc.
Kodak, Tennessee 37764
Virginia Beach, Virginia 23462

SMOKY MOUNTAIN MYSTERIES, Copyright © 2002
by Alma Juanitta Stallcup Baldwin

All rights reserved. Without limiting the rights reserved under the copyrights for this book, no part of this book may be reproduced by any method which now exists or may exist in the future, or introduced into any storage and/or retrieval system, or transmitted by any method without prior written permission of the copyright owner. Reviewers may quote brief excerpts.

Although the author has researched all available sources to produce complete and accurate information, she assumes no responsibility for errors, inaccuracies, omissions, or any inconsistency. The dialogues used in the stories, in some instances, are constructed from oral history and written records. The author interviewed people who were either alive at the time and place about which reported and have personal memories or shared what they heard. The dialogues represent the essence of how persons spoke at the time and place of the event. No distinction is made between actual dialogue and constructed dialogue.

Anything that anyone may interpret as a slight is absolutely unintentional.

Printed and bound in the United States of America
First Printing 2002

Library of Congress Catalog Card Number: 2002090194

ISBN 1880308-18-5

# TABLE OF CONTENTS

| | |
|---|---|
| Chapter 1 — Why Are the Mountains Smoky? | 7 |
| Chapter 2 — Sandy's Frolicking Ghost | 14 |
| Chapter 3 — Unexplained Balds — Majestic Vantage Points | 28 |
| Chapter 4 — Ghosts Dance on Hazel Creek | 37 |
| Chapter 5 — An Enigma — Bells Hanging in Trees | 54 |
| Chapter 6 — The Sinks — A Place of Myth and Mystery | 58 |
| Chapter 7 — Lone Grave Marker — A Story About the White Caps and Blue Bills | 65 |
| Chapter 8 — Who Wrote on Judaculla Rock? | 82 |
| Chapter 9 — Riddle of the Brown Mountain Lights | 86 |
| Chapter 10 — Whose Bones Were in Our Barn? | 97 |
| Chapter 11 — Melungeons — People of Mystery | 114 |
| Chapter 12 — Fairy Cross/Cross Stone — Facts, Folklore and Legends About It | 126 |
| Chapter 13 — Sarbe Springs Haints | 135 |
| Chapter 14 — Do Angels Sing on Roan Mountain? | 142 |
| Chapter 15 — Mysterious Mounds | 152 |

*This book is dedicated to
my husband,
Jesse Baldwin,
for his help and patience!*

I also thank everyone who contributed to this book by allowing me to review and use documents and photographs, and for sharing personal experiences.

I enjoy hearing from my readers.

- E-mail: juanittabaldwin@authorsden.com

- Regular mail: PO Box 98, Kodak, TN 37764

- Website: http://www.juanittabaldwin.com

# Chapter 1
# Why Are the Mountains Smoky?

Blue smoke drifts and swirls across the magnificent mountains in Southern Appalachia most of the time.

Watching it is akin to watching a master painter with a brush and a canvas. The painting looks beautiful and complete to the untrained eye, but as the artist adds a wisp here and there, it takes on greater perfection.

And so it is with the blue smoke. The mountains are the canvas, Nature is the painter, and everyone is invited to enjoy the living art. It changes constantly, and only on rare occasions does Nature put away the smoke brush and allow the sun, or moon, to have full sway with the mountains.

Photo by Juanitta Baldwin —View from my front porch

The smoke has inspired many names for the mountains within the Appalachian Range — the Great Blue Hills of God, Great Smoky Mountains, Blue Ridge Mountains, and Shaconage, the Cherokee word that translates into English as "the place of the blue smoke."

When I first became curious about the origin/cause of the blue smoke, I asked a modern-day scientist and a folklorist who is steeped in Cherokee history and culture.

The scientist prefers the term "blue haze," because the phenomenon is not *real* smoke. The basic explanation is that the air that surrounds the Earth is a colorless, odorless, tasteless gas. The air is colored blue when violet and blue lightwaves are scattered by small molecules.

Not being a scientist, the best I could do to get the gist of what causes blue haze was to imagine a happy dance between molecules and light. More about this later.

The folklorist answered my question about the blue smoke by telling two enchanting legends the Cherokees developed to explain it.

### The Legend of Nunnehi Underground Fires

The Cherokees, the first people known to inhabit the smoky mountains, were keen observers. They understood how interconnected animate and inanimate things are.

They used fire and understood the basic operation of it. They observed the natural law that where there is smoke, there is fire. Logic told them the smoke that spread across the mountains came from a fire, and they searched for it.

But they could not locate the place where fire was burning. Then they decided there were many fires, and they were coming from the underground homes of the Nunnehi — a race of spirit people, also called immortals and fairies — who also inhabited the smoky mountains at that time.

The two races respected each other and lived in harmony. Many people believe the Nunnehi still live in the smoky mountains, and appear at will.

Huge man-made earthen mounds had been built before the Cherokees arrived, and they came to believe that some Nunnehi lived deep within the mounds. Those who did not live in mounds made underground homes in sheltered valleys, sometimes under flowing water.

Nunnehi homes have a fireplace. Smoke from the fires rises into the air, and the wind spreads it across the mountains.

And that explains the origin of the blue smoke!

### A Bit About the Nunnehi

The Nunnehi have the ability to make themselves visible or invisible to humans. When they choose to be visible they take on the characteristics of the people with whom they are mingling at the time.

The Nunnehi love music and dance. The Cherokees would hear their music but could never find the source of it unless the Nunnehi became visible and invited them to join in their festivities.

On occasion, the Nunnehi would make themselves visible and join in Cherokee dancing. The Cherokee dancers would accept the strangers, thinking they were from another tribe. But after the dance ended, they would leave.

There are many legends of braves trying to track beautiful maidens to whom they were attracted. The maidens would play the game, but always stayed ahead of their trackers. The Nunnehi ended the game by making themselves invisible.

## The Legend of Grandmother Spider

Creatures who first inhabited the mountains knew that the magnificent peaks and valleys had been formed by one of their own when the Earth was young and soft.

One day Nature had allowed a Great Buzzard, with a giant wingspan, to fly at great speed. He pulled up the mountains by flapping his wings up, and the valleys by flapping his wings down. He soared back and forth until Nature approved his handiwork.

The creatures — animals, fish, birds, insects, and a few plants — loved the mountains and the valleys, but there was no light at the time. They grew weary of the darkness, and often talked about how much better things would be if they had a sun like the creatures had on the other side of the world that gave light, and fire that gave warmth.

One day Wolf called a meeting to figure out how to get light and warmth from the sun on the other side of the world. Coyote suggested that the Moles dig a tunnel to the other side of the world so the sun could shine through it.

They pondered this for a while and decided that the Moles could dig a tunnel, and another creature would crawl through it and bring back a piece of the sun.

The Moles toiled for many months. One day they told the creatures that they had finished digging a tunnel to the other side of the world, and had seen the sun.

Grandmother Spider was the first to volunteer to crawl through the tunnel and bring back a piece of the sun.

But the other creatures thought she was too old to go. Being very wise she did not protest, just watched, prepared a plan, and waited.

Wolf, Coyote, Rabbit, and all other animals with fur who tried to bring a piece of the sun from the other side of the world caught fire. Their lives were saved by other creatures pouring water over them and snuffing out the fire. And, one by one, all the animals who tried to bring the fire through the tunnel failed for one reason or another.

The creatures were so desperate that they asked Grandmother Spider to go, and she readily agreed, because she had prepared for the journey. She had molded a small clay pot and placed it on her back. When she was ready to go, she filled it with water, grass and sticks.

The water would evaporate from the bowl during her long crawl, but it would keep the bowl moist enough so it would not become brittle and crack from the heat of the fire. The grass and sticks would be dry enough to keep the fire alive during her crawl back through the tunnel.

### Grandmother Spider's Journey

When Grandmother Spider got to the other side of the world, the creatures who lived there greeted her with kindness. The spiders helped her spin a web so she could crawl up to where the sun was resting on the top of a mountain.

Grandmother Spider smiled, and the sun bent toward her. She broke off a small piece of fire and put it in her clay pot. After thanking the sun and the spiders, she crawled back to her side of the world with the fire.

All the creatures ran to greet her. Wolf threw a piece of the fire into air, and Nature turned it into a sun. From that day on, their side of the world was warm and bright.

The creatures met to celebrate and honor Grandmother Spider. Nature bestowed a great honor upon her by redesigning the anatomy of her species of spider to include a small pot on their back. Her descendants carry this pot to this day.

The creatures told the Moles to close the tunnel, but Grandmother Spider could not let this be done. She told them that the sun on the other side of the world might go out, and the creatures who lived there would need to crawl though the tunnel to get fire.

Grandmother Spider told them that she would weave a strong web over the entrance to the tunnel to mark the spot, and to protect it. The creatures agreed, and watched her weave the web.

Grandmother Spider did not tell the other creatures that she had dropped bits of fire into the tunnel, and it was smoldering.

She had decided to do this while she was on the other side of the world.

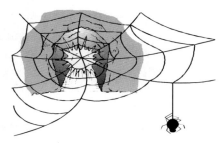

As she had climbed up to where the sun had been resting, she saw that fire was burning on black rocks that were like some of the rocks in the tunnel between the two sides of the world. If the fire went out on either side of the world, they could get fire from the tunnel. It would be hidden by the thick web she had woven over the entrance to the tunnel.

All the creatures, except Grandmother Spider, were puzzled when blue smoke drifted over the mountains from places where there was no fire. One day whispered she secret into the ear of a Cherokee.

### Scientific Explanations of Blue Smoke

The scientific molecular theory is the basis for the all the theories about the blue smoke over the mountains. This theory is that all matter consists of molecules which are in constant motion, and are held together by molecular forces. In a solid, a huge number of molecules are packed tightly together and their range of motion consists largely of oscillations around points of equilibrium.

The air that surrounds the earth is a colorless, odorless and tasteless gas, with freewheeling molecules.

Scientists theorize that hydrogen and carbon boil off in vapor form from trees and other types of vegetation. The rays from the sun causes the vapors to interact with each other and other elements to built particles. The particles grow large and scatter blue light, and presto: blue haze—blue smoke!

Logic tells me that the scientists are probably correct. But sometimes when I am walking in blue smoke, I wonder...

- *Is this smoke from Nunnehi fireplaces?*

- *Is this smoke from the tunnel to the other side of the world?*

## Chapter 2
## Sandy's Frolicking Ghost

When Sandy and Jeff McCarter were looking for a house, they knew they wanted an older home in Sevierville, Tennessee. They had settled on the acceptable size of the lot, the number of bedrooms and bathrooms, and other specifications for the house. After looking for a while, they found the right house and bought it in 1985.

Photo courtesy Sandy and Jeff McCarter

The McCarters had not specified that the house must have a resident ghost, so when one showed up that was a big shock. After the shock wore off, and they got to know their ghost, Sandy began to consider him her frolicking ghost. Jeff has yet to accept him as a member of the household.

Sandy laughs, "We're the only ones in our family, or circle of friends, who can entertain 'believers' and 'doubting Thomases' with true, ongoing ghost tales!"

"Jeff does not want to think we host a ghost. But he cannot explain all the strange goings-on. Trenton, our young son, is not frightened, and just reacts to noises our ghost makes with about the same degree of attention and curiosity as when he hears one of us making a noise. Neither of us has ever seen a ghost, but we've all seen him move objects!"

### First Encounter — Phantom Footsteps

The first encounter Sandy and Jeff had with their resident ghost involved hearing phantom footsteps, but not at the same time.

Sandy recalls the first time she heard phantom footsteps. "Not long after we moved into our home, I was alone in the house one afternoon, working downstairs. Suddenly I became aware of footsteps overhead. I stopped and listened, feeling apprehensive because no one should be upstairs.

"The footsteps seemed to pace from one room to another, and sounded like a man wearing heavy boots. After what seemed like an eternity, I got up the courage to go upstairs and take a look. The cadence slowed, but the footsteps continued as I went up the stairs. They stopped abruptly as I reached the top step.

"There was no way for a person to get out of the upstairs without my seeing or hearing them. I tiptoed around gingerly and looked everywhere. There was no one anywhere, and nothing was out of place. Whoever, or whatever, had been walking upstairs had simply vanished!

"I could not explain what had happened to myself, so I did not tell Jeff at that point. But I kept hearing the footsteps, and gradually my apprehension evaporated. I began to toy with the possibility that what I was hearing was a ghost.

"I'd probably never have thought it could be a ghost if it had not been for an experience my grandfather told me about.

"Grandpa said that one night he was walking alone across a field near some woods, not far from his home. Suddenly he felt someone grab him from behind and hold him in a tight bear hug. He thought it was his brother trying to scare him, but when he was able to look around no one was there.

"He said he was scared and lit out across the field for home. He never knew what happened, but he never scoffed at the idea of ghosts after that!

"I was thankful that whoever, or whatever, was producing the sound of footsteps had not hugged me! I've heard stories about ghosts all my life, and took most of them with a grain of salt. But after so many months of hearing footsteps, I was like my grandfather. I didn't know what was happening, but I no longer rejected the idea that ghosts exist. Also, I was more inclined to accept the presence of a ghost rather than to go get my head examined!

"I finally told Jeff about the footsteps, and my theory. Being skeptical to the bone, he laughed at the idea that we had a ghost walking around.

"I was confident he would hear them eventually, and told him so. He said, 'That will never happen!' Jeff's skepticism made me decide to wait until he heard the footsteps before I tried to identify who the ghost had been in life."

### Jeff Heard Our Ghost Walking

After a few months Jeff heard the footsteps. Sandy recalls, "One morning he asked me what I was doing upstairs to walk around so much last night. I told him it was not me, it was our ghost. He thought I was putting him on, but I was adamant that I was downstairs. He insisted he'd heard footsteps.

"I suggested that he had just imagined hearing footsteps like he told me I did. That left Jeff between a rock and a hard place. He did not want to think he'd imagined the footsteps, and he could not bring himself to think he'd heard a ghost walking! He still hears the sound that resembles 'footsteps,' and is still trying to come up with a logical explanation.

"At that point in time I had no idea that walking was just the first act in our ghost's repertoire!"

### Sheer Terror

I remarked to Sandy that I'd probably be terrified, and marveled at the whole family's composure.

"Our ghost has terrified me only one time," she said, and opened her eyes wide at the memory. "Trenton had a science project to observe how weathering smooths rock. To demonstrate this, the students were to take small rough rocks and rotate them in a machine until they were smooth.

"We bought the little machine at Wal-Mart, filled it with small rocks and turned it on. It made an awful racket that could be heard all over the house. The estimated time for it to smooth the rocks was two weeks if it ran continuously.

"We put it in the little room upstairs with the window that faces the street. There were curtains on a rod above the window, and they were open.

"One afternoon Trenton and I came home and the machine was not running. I thought the power had gone off, but I flipped on a light switch and the power was on. We went upstairs to check, and the machine was unplugged.

"There was a small table in the room, and it was overturned so that the leg was across the cord. I did not think there was enough vibration from the machine to have done this, so I plugged in the cord and turned the table over. The cord stayed in the socket. I did this about six times with the same result. By then I was feeling queasy but did not say anything to Trenton, of course.

"Trenton turned on the machine and we left the room. During the next few days it stopped several times. Trenton or I would go turn it back on, and neither of us saw anything to explain why it had been turned off.

"The machine had been running off and on for about a week when terror struck. We came home late in the afternoon, and the back door was standing wide open. Trenton said the machine was not running. Jeff was out of town.

"When we went in, there were muddy footprints all though the house and up the stairs to the room where the machine was supposed to be running. When we walked into the room, the curtain rod, with the curtains still on it, was crumpled in a heap on the floor.

"Then the light dawned! Our ghost did not like the noise the machine was making day and night. I stood right there and explained, in a loud and impatient tone, that this was a science project that had to be completed, and the more the machine was unplugged, the longer it would have to run. I concluded by asking, 'Please, whoever you are, or were, leave it alone!'

"Trenton just took it in stride, but my nerves were shot. I was terrified. He turned on the machine, I locked the house, and we went to my parents' home and spent the night.

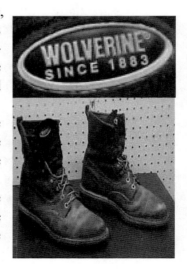

"I got up my courage and we returned home the next day. The machine was running and the muddy footprints were still there.

"On closer examination, the footprints looked like they were made with boots like this vintage pair.

"After this twilight zone experience, I decided it was time to try to find out who the person, or persons, had been in life.

"It seemed logical that the ghost would be someone who had lived in the house. It also seemed logical that the ghost was a man, because the footsteps always sounded like a man wearing heavy boots, and he'd left muddy footprints!"

### The History of Our Haunted House

I asked Sandy if the seller had said anything that might hint that the house was haunted.

"No, he didn't. We found our house through an advertisement in the "Houses for Sale" section of the local newspaper. We drove by and saw that it was vacant, and looked around outside. We liked it, and called the contact person. That person turned out to be a relative of the last person to own and live in the house, Mrs. Willie G. McMahan. She had bought the house in 1982 from Rosemary and James McAfee and lived there until she died in 1984.

"This was enough to check the official records and find the names of everybody who had owned it. The fellow who handled the sale said it was built around 1918.

"Official records at the Sevier County Courthouse show that Mr. A.J. Nave bought the lot, on which our home now stands, on the third of July 1920, for $100.00, from C.A. Kyker and C.L. Thurman. He built a two-story house with an attic on it, and he and his wife, Mabel, lived there until he died in 1925.

"Several of the Murphy College catalogues on display in the Sevier County Library list Professor A.J. Nave as the teacher for English and Preparatory Work.

"The Tennessee State Library and Archives, Historical and Genealogical Information Record #227, shows that NAVE, A.J., died in 1925, at age 48. The cause of death was botulism. He contracted it from eating in the lunch room at Murphy College. A lot of other people died in the outbreak.

"This is a picture of the Murphy College Administration Building from the college catalogue for 1913-1914. The building still stands, and is in use in Sevierville in 2002.

"Professor Nave's widow, Mabel, owned the house until 1944 when she sold it to Rosemary and James McAfee. As I mentioned earlier, the McAfees sold it Mrs. Willie G. McMahan."

### Our Ghost's Identity

Sandy says, "With this information about the previous owners of our house, I concluded that Professor A.J. Nave is our primary resident ghost. I say "primary resident ghost" because I do not wish to offend any of the others — if there are others!

"I feel sad to know that he got to live in his house for such a short time. He built a new house on a street that was, at that time, probably the most fashionable neighborhood in Sevierville and got to live in it less than five years before he died. The population of Sevierville was about 800, and he could walk to the college.

"Although distance is probably irrelevant to a ghost, sometimes when I am awakened by footsteps, I suggest to the good Professor that he go over and check on things at the college!

"Jeff's experiences now make him think that there may be more than one ghost. His nomination for primary ghost is Mrs. Willie McMahan because his most vivid experience with our ghost was in the room we now use as a dining room. When Mrs. McMahan lived in the house, she used it as a bedroom and that is where she died."

When I asked Jeff about this, he said, "I cannot explain the noises we hear, and if there is such a thing as ghosts, we have more than one. I have also learned that Mrs. McMahan had someone living in the house who had a pet monkey. Maybe the monkey and its owner are still 'monkeying around!' "

Sandy and Jeff both agree that if we are hosting ghosts, so be it. So far all of them have been benevolent. They love their home, and have no plans to move. If the ghosts do move, they will miss them!

### More Evidence

Sandy says that, "In addition to the boot footsteps, I think it is Professor Nave because when we opened the crawl space to the attic while we were remodeling, we found it was crammed full of old lard buckets and similar stuff, dating back to the 1920s! They had to have been put there by Professor Nave or his family.

"Since no one had bothered Professor Nave's stash of lard buckets and similar stuff, and no one else left anything in the house to come back and protect or examine, he's the only one who left property on our premises! Maybe he stored some great treasure in them, but we have yet to find it."

Sandy said, "We decided to tell this story because the strange goings-on in our house are a real part of our daily life. And so many ghost stories strike fear in our hearts. Our ghost just goes to prove that not all ghosts are the same. Jeff, Trenton and I lead lives very similar to our peers, except for our ghost(s)! Jeff and I hold responsible professional jobs in the business world, and Trenton goes to school."

### Our Ghost Walks When He Wants To!

I asked Sandy where the ghost walks. She laughed and told me, "Wherever he wants to, I suppose. After several months of listening to the footsteps overhead, I realized they were not random. The footsteps begin anywhere upstairs, and walk around, but always go into the room where Jeff has his computer. I think Professor Nave is trying to figure out what this contraption is, or maybe he's trying to learn to use it!

"There is no particular time for him to take a walk. He walks during the day and at night. So far, we've heard him only when we are downstairs. The footsteps are upstairs. The footsteps are sort of routine now, but he gets spells when all kinds of things go on."

### Playing With Trenton's Lamp

I felt the hair on the back of my neck stand up, and asked, "What kind of things?"

Sandy chucked at my obvious lack of courage. "Well, we really had a round one night when the Professor decided to play with Trenton's lamp.

"I always keep a touch lamp in Trenton's bedroom, and always keep it on the low setting. One night he was having a problem going to sleep. I lay down beside him on his bed to comfort him.

"The moment I was prone on the bed, the lamp went up to the highest level of brightness. I got up and turned it down to where it needed to be.

"As soon as I lay back down it went right back up to the highest level again! I got up again and turned it down again. Once again, as soon as I lay down it went right back to the highest level.

"Before I could get out of bed to touch it, it started going back and forth from low to high. I was frustrated and hollered for Jeff. 'Jeff, get in here! Something is wrong with this lamp.'

"Jeff came in, and you guessed it, the lamp stayed on its proper setting the whole time he was in the room. Evidently the professor just wanted to play with Trenton and me!

"This episode was the only one with lights that has happened while anyone was in a room. But so many times, when Trenton has an asthma attack, I will sleep on the couch. I've seen the lights come on and go off upstairs, and heard old music playing, like it is coming from an old Victrola. This happens when no one is upstairs, and we do not own an old Victrola and have not found one anywhere in the house!"

### Our Ghost Opened a Blind!

"One afternoon I was sitting by the window in my recliner reading a book. I keep my blinds closed all the time because our lot is small. A rattling noise began in the blind beside my chair. It sounded like there might be a fly or bug buzzing between the blind and the window.

"When I looked over at the blind, the wand that you use to open and close the slats moved straight out to an almost vertical position. I watched in disbelief as the blind opened!

"Within a few seconds, the wand fell back into its normal position against the blind, and the slats were open!

"Needless to say, I did not move — for a few minutes. Maybe, to be more accurate, I *could* not move for a few minutes!

"When I finally did move, I said, 'Okay, if you want the blind open, that's fine. We'll leave it that way.' And I did the rest of the day!

"When I closed the blind, I stood still for a few minutes to see if the Professor would open it again. Thankfully, he didn't!"

### Flying Candy

"Right after Valentine's Day several years back, Jeff had his most active encounter with our ghost. I had bought him a lot of that hot red candy that comes in big pieces and wrapped in red cellophane.

"One afternoon Jeff and I had a kind of heated discussion. I went and sat down in the living room.

"As he was walking through the dining room a piece of that red hot candy flew across the room and hit him!

"He looked at me and demanded, 'Who threw that?'

"I just died laughing, and told him, 'You see I'm sitting in the the living room, and that candy came from the opposite side of the house. Maybe our ghost threw it to let you know I'm right!'

"Jeff turned a few colors over that. He knew I could not have thrown it, and he still can't explain that flying candy."

### Trenton's Push Toy

I asked Sandy if Trenton has experiences with the ghost when he is alone.

"We don't know," she said. "Remember, the ghost was there before Trenton was born, and some of the stuff that goes on just seems normal to him since he's never lived in a "ghost-free" house! Trenton and I had a bad episode one night when he decided to play with Trenton's push toy."

I asked her to tell me about it.

Sandy said, "He really misbehaved that night! I'd have given him an eviction notice if I could! This is what he did. At that time, Trenton had a toy that made a noise when you push it, and it was under his bed at the time.

"It was his bedtime, but he was having problems settling down because of his asthma, so I had lain down beside him. He had just settled down when the noise from that push toy went off.

"We were both prone on the bed and there is no way either of us could have reached under the bed and touched it.

"I thought, 'How about that,' but lay still. In a few minutes it went off again. Then I said in the same stern voice I use with Trenton when he's trying my patience, 'Whoever you are, quit playing with that toy!'

"That must have aggravated our ghost because he hit that toy four or five times, making it go off with the loudest racket it could possibly make.

"That racket had to stop, so I got out of bed, got down on my hands and knees, and crawled up under the bed — half afraid of what I was going to find when I got it out.

"I was tired and exasperated with our ghost that night, so I marched right to the back door and threw the toy as far as I could into the back yard. I yelled, 'If you want to play with that toy, you go out back and play with it. We're trying to sleep, so leave us alone.' I hope the neighbors did not hear me!

"I thought about it later and I think that the Professor just wanted to play with Trenton and me. I even wondered if I'd hurt his feelings because it was peaceful the rest of the night, and we did not have any other encounters for a several months! But he came back, and life goes on with my frolicking ghost!

"As they say — stay tuned!"

## There Is *Difference* Between a *Ghost* and a *Haint*!

In the South — and that is where Sevierville, Tennessee, is — folks talk about haints. Of course, technically, some folks say "haint" is just an old-fashioned word for "ghost."

But I beg to differ, because Southerners who know about these things tell me that anybody who encounters a "haint" will know the difference!

A *ghost* is an indefinable something that causes odd things to happen — like playing a Victrola, turning off a rock-smoothing machine, walking around and leaving muddy footprints.

A *haint* is an overwhelming force that scares the bejeevers out of people.

So far, the ghosts in the McCarter home have behaved like ghosts with an attitude, not like haints!

But, as Sandy says, "Stay tuned!"

## Chapter 3
## Unexplained Balds — Majestic Vantage Points

There are about 80 unexplained upland grassy areas in the forests of southern Appalachia. These areas are called balds, because when this word is applied to terrain it means "the absence of the usual or natural covering."

The natural covering would be a forest with large trees, but they are covered thick grass, wildflowers and small bushes. And herein lies the unexplained. There is much debate about how they were created. There is, however, no debate that they are majestic vantage points.

Photo courtesy of Richard Weisser and smokyphotos.com

This is a view from Andrews Bald, the highest bald in the Great Smoky Mountains, about 5900 feet. It is about two miles from the Clingmans Dome parking lot. The trail is well marked and maintained, but very rocky. The climb up to the open field is steep, but if you hang in there you will find yourself at the center of a circular stage. At this point you'll wish for 360-degree vision!

### Arguments and Legends About the Origin of the Balds

There are three major scientific arguments by experts about the origin of the balds.

- **The Nature Argument** — Nature created them, perhaps by fires started by lightning or high acidity in the soil, and the huge animal population kept them free of trees.
- **The Cherokee Argument** — The balds were created when the forests were cleared by the Cherokees, or by the people who populated the land before them, and deer, elk and other animals inhibited regrowth.

The Cherokees have no oral history of having done this. The major flaw in this argument is ample archeological evidence that they generally lived in the valleys, near rivers and streams, avoiding the inhospitable climate at high altitudes.

- **Early Settlers Argument** — The balds are simply patches that early settlers cleared in the forests, after taking the land from the Cherokees, to graze their cattle, but there are no records of who cleared mountaintops on such an extensive scale, or when.

Records show that the settlers did graze their herds in the balds and enlarged them as their herds grew. In the late 19th and early 20th centuries, Tennessee and North Carolina farmers herded thousands of cattle, sheep, mules and horses to the balds in spring and brought them down about Labor Day.

Gregory Bald, whom some proclaim has the most extraordinary deciduous azaleas on earth, got its name from Russell Gregory. He and his family moved to the bald in the 1820s, and lived there for about seven years.

The National Park Service banned cattle grazing in the park after 1934, and on some of the balds vegetation, shrubs, and trees are closing in. The Park Service has decided to preserve some of them in as natural a state as possible.

- **Legend of the Devil's Footsteps** — The Devil walked in the mountains, and the balds are his footsteps.
- **Legend of the Catawba Battles** — This legend explains how the balds on Roan Mountain were created and why the rhododendron that grow on it are crimson.

This legend is in the book, *Adventures in the wilds of the United States and British American provinces*, by Charles Lanman, published in 1856.

"There was once a time when all the nations of the earth were at war with the Catawbas, and had proclaimed their determination to conquer and possess their country.

"On hearing this intelligence the Catawbas became greatly enraged, and sent a challenge to all their enemies, and dared them to a fight on the summit of the Roan.

"The challenge was accepted, and no less than three famous battles were fought. The streams of the entire land were red with blood, a number of tribes became extinct, and the Catawbas carried the day.

"Whereupon it was that the Great Spirit caused the forests to wither from the three peaks of the Roan Mountain where the battles were fought; and wherefore it is that the flowers which grow upon this mountain are chiefly of a crimson hue, for they are nourished by the blood of the slain."

### Wildflowers on the Balds

One of the unique attractions of the balds are blooming plants. Three of the most prolific wild plants are rhododendron, mountain laurel, and azalea. They bloom on the balds, and at lower elevations from May through late summer.

## Rhododendron

Rhododendrons are prolific at all elevations. They bloom in early summer, and put on quite a show, with flower clusters of 5 to 6 inches in hues of white, purple and crimson.

Photograph courtesy of Richard Weisser and smokyphotos.com

Rhododendron leaves are dark green, thick, and leathery. Leaves get "old and tired" and drop off at any time of the year. New ones appear during the active growing season

Rhododendron often grows in patches that are so thick that humans find them almost impenetrable  Botanists classify such patches as "heath balds." Mountain laurel also grows so thick it forms "heath balds."

Native mountaineers often call the heath balds "laurel hells," — whether the plants are laurel or rhododendron — because if people wander into them it is almost impossible to walk out. The only way to escape is to crawl out.

Bears can easily navigate the heath balds, and they use them as safe havens.

## Mountain Laurel

Mountain laurel blooms are somewhat similar to Rhododendron, but generally smaller. The colors range from pure white to deep raspberry pink. The leaves are smaller and less leathery than the rhododendron.

Mountain laurel has the distinction of having many common names. Among them are Calico bush, American laurel, Broad-leafed laurel, Sheep laurel, and Spoonwood.

My favorite common name for the mountain laurel is "Calico," because a childhood friend and I played under a "Callico tree." Many years later, I wrote a novel and titled it *The Callico Tree*.

The cover was to picture a single mountain laurel loaded with clusters of pink blooms. After my publisher and I searched in vain for a photograph, I persuaded my husband, Jesse, to take on the job. We searched from early morning until about 4 p.m. without finding a mountain laurel that stood alone — that we could get to. Most were in clusters, or on steep banks like this one beside a rushing stream.

Photograph by Jesse Baldwin

We found several beautiful rhododendrons growing alone. With his stamina, and patience, wearing thin, Jesse suggested wearily, "Just change the title to *The Rhododendron Tree*, and let's go home!" Of course, that would never do!

We limped on, our psyches hanging by a thread. An hour later, we rounded a curve and *Voila!* — there stood the perfect callico tree almost overwhelmed with pink flowers!

## Azalea

Gregory Bald, elevation 4949 feet, is a prime destination for azalea lovers. These are not the demur azaleas that grow in back yards. They reach toward the sky as high as 15 feet, and usually bloom in June. There is a dazzling assortment of colors, from pure white to deep orange-red.

Many of the native mountaineers call the azalea "honeysuckle bush." The blooms are similar to the common honeysuckle vine, but generally they are larger and more vivid.

Photograph courtesy of Richard Weisser and smokyphotos.com

Gregory Bald is a long walk, about 11 miles, from the nearest place in Cades Cove where you can park your car, but do not despair — there are azaleas on other balds, and in places on the mountains that can be seen from your car.

Andrews Bald, about 2 miles from the Clingmans Dome parking lot also has a great wild azalea garden.

### Longest Balds in the World

Roan Mountain is almost as high as the Smokies, but significantly farther north, and some scientists compare its ecosystem to one normally found in Canada. It supports a more northern species of plants and animals.

It is crowned with 10 miles of grassy balds, the longest stretch of balds in the world. Jane Bald, Hump and Little Hump mountains, and Grassy Ridge make up the largest of the southern Appalachian grass balds.

The Roan hosts a potpourri of wildflowers and rare plants, including the Greys Lily, a relic from the ice age. But the most famous plant is the Catawba rhododendron, which grows in one of the world's largest natural rhododendron "gardens."

Visitors to Roan Mountain balds today see much of what Dr. Elisha Mitchell saw in 1827 and 1828 when he made a geological tour of the mountain

The impressions of those tours remained strong, and in 1836, he wrote, "The top of the Roan may be described as a vast meadow without a tree to obstruct this prospect, where a person may gallop his horse for a mile or two with Carolina at his feet on one side and Tennessee on the other, and a green ocean of mountains rising in tremendous billows immediately around him."

And Mike Calabrese found the same vastness in mid-April 1999, when he hiked the Roan. He said it was bitter cold and

Photo courtesy Mike Calabrese — mikecalabrese@mikecalabrese.com

spitting snow the day this picture was made. Mike was hiking alone. He met a couple on their honeymoon and they snapped this picture of him on Jane's Bald, near Carver Gap.

You can read his account of hiking on the Appalachian Trailon his Website — http://www.mikecalabrese.com.

**Jane's Bald is Roan Mountain's Most Famous Bald**

Jane's Bald is named for Jane Cook, one of George Cook's 21 children. In the 1870s she lived near Dogwood Flats, on the North Carolina side of Roan Mountain.

In November 1870 Jane and her sister Harriet went to visit two of their sisters who lived in Carter County on the Tennessee side, walking all the way there and back.

They started home on the morning of November 16, under blue skies and moderate temperature. They had to cross the Roan Highlands, and before they got across the wind began to howl, clouds moved in and the temperature dropped.

Harriet had been seriously ill during the summer. Her strength gave out and she collapsed. Harriet stopped talking, but Jane did not dare move until daylight.

As the sun came up, she rushed to the home of Charley Young, who lived close to Carver's Gap. He and several other men rescued Harriet from the mountain. Harriet died within hours, but Jane survived until the 1940s.

People began to call the place where Jane and Harriet had their ordeal Jane's Bald. At some point it became official.

The source of this story is the March 29, 1999, issue of the Johnson City Press, Johnson City, Tennessee.

### The Balds Are Wild Places

The balds are the focus of inquisitive minds. But never forget they are wild places.

Looking into the Sun on Andrews Bald — 9/04/1999
Photograph courtesy Vince Bishop

## Chapter 4
## Ghosts Dance on Hazel Creek

Until Saturday, October 10, 1885, Lucius and Almarine Kinsland, mature and God-fearing people, had believed that the Holy Ghost was the *only* ghost. Thereafter, they *knew* there were at least five other ghosts, because they had seen them dance and heard them speak.

It happened before dawn. Lucius and Almarine lit lanterns, picked up zinc buckets, and set off over a path up the hill to the milk gap. There was a nip in the air, and a heavy mist hung over the tops of the Smoky Mountains surrounding their log home on Hazel Creek in North Carolina.

The whippoorwills and rain crows were calling loud enough to be heard above the roar of Hazel Creek at the bottom of the hill.

Their two cows were at the gap, eager for the handful of middlings to chomp while they were being milked. They lifted the milking stools over the split rail fence and began to milk.

Lucius had zigzagged a couple of streams of milk into the bucket, when Almarine heard him stop, stand up and knock the stool over. She called out, "What's wrong?"

Lucius did not answer. Alarmed, Almarine stopped milking, rose from her stool, and looked over the cow's back. The first rays of the sun made it possible for her to see that he was staring hypnotically toward the entrance to their closed copper mine about a hundred feet away. She looked in that direction, but saw nothing unusual. "Lucius, what do you see?"

No answer. A cerebral blast of concern and rage rang through Almarine. She set her bucket down and demanded as she scurried toward him, "Are you sick? Answer me!"

The sun popped over the ridge behind them. Lucius pointed toward the mine. A muffled sound came from that direction. Almarine turned and thought she saw people standing in a circle atop the debris from the landslide that had closed the entrance to the mine. They were diaphanous, and appeared to be moving. She wanted to think the rocks were reflecting the sun, but her shrewd eyes would not permit deception.

Before she could speak, Lucius said in a tone rife with terror, "I know Uncle John and the others are dead, but I see them. Can you see them?"

She nodded. They clasped their arms around each other, transfixed in bewildered trepidation. The muffled sound faded.

Uncle John, with his fiddle at the ready, materialized on the rock ledge overhanging the entrance to the mine.

They saw him draw the bow over the strings, then "Turkey in the Straw" vibrated loud and clear through the air.

Then they heard his familiar chant,

"Find your partners and promenade!"

The diaphanous bodies solidified, found their partners and formed a square. After a few seconds Lucius and Almarine recognized all of them! But this could not be! They had been buried beneath the debris upon they were now dancing on that fateful night the previous July.

Uncle John called, "Allemande your left! All at home, fall in line."

The dance began, and they heard the familiar laughter of people they had seen die in a landslide.

Almarine whispered, "Are we having a nightmare? I know these people are dead, and I don't believe in ghosts."

As if to answer, Uncle John called, "Promenade and circulate, swing your lady, like swinging a gate!"

Lucius shuddered. "I don't know! And I'm cold sober. It's broad daylight, and I see dead people dancing. Maybe the Rapture has come like the Bible says, the dead have risen, and we've all been caught up in the air on our way to Heaven or Hell!"

The fiddle fell silent, the voices got thinner and thinner, and finally they died away. Almarine released Lucius from her grip and looked down the hill. Hazel Creek was high with flood water. The banks were rimmed with the golden leaves of witch hazel bushes, but there were no streets of gold. "We're still on Hazel Creek," she announced with great relief.

Lucius shouted, "Thank God! What happened?"

Almarine knew one thing suddenly and clearly. She had seen five ghosts, and was alive to tell the tale. "We saw the ghosts of Uncle John, Melvin and Joleen Rister, Ennis Cartwell and Louise Wiggins," she said, as her eyes rimmed with tears. "Let's go to the house and talk about it. I didn't notice when the cows left, but I don't feel like going through the wet weeds to hunt them. And besides, I'm hungry."

"Let's do that," he said, pulling his watch out of his pocket. "My God! It's almost nine o'clock."

### Journal Entries

The biscuits were burned, and the fire in the cook stove had gone out. Lucius got the fire going, and Almarine put a new batch of biscuits in the oven. She fried fatback, and Lucius made coffee. When the biscuits were almost brown, she scrambled a dozen eggs.

As she put the food on the table, she announced, "This is breakfast, and dinner, and maybe supper! I want to talk out what happened this morning, and write it down. We'll go over it and agree on what we saw, and I'll write it as we go along."

"Okay. I'll keep your pencils sharp. I'd planned to cut some firewood today, but I'm so wrung out I might hack my foot off. It's a good idea to write it down, because I'm already wondering exactly what I saw. If you hadn't been up there, and I had seen them, I don't know if I would ever have told it or not. You'd think I was either drunk or making it up."

"Probably," she conceded. "And if I had been up there by myself, I might have fainted. I have never been so mystified or terrified. What do you think our children and our kinfolks will say when we tell them?"

Lucius laughed hard as he thought about his family. "The young'uns will think we're crazy. Mama will gloat because she's told us for years that she sees ghosts. Old Preacher Buck Flaughtery will call us sinners and shout for us to come to the altar and confess because God is merciful to backsliders who have been cavorting with the Devil."

Images of past encounters with Preacher Flaughtery that had left her exhausted flashed though Almarine's head. "Maybe we ought not to tell anybody for a little while," she said. "People bring flowers to the mine all the time. Somebody else may see them and tell us."

Lucius grinned, "That sounds like a good and sane idea, but we'll bust if we don't tell!"

While Almarine washed the breakfast dishes, Lucius got their journal and three pencils from the cedar chest and laid them on the kitchen table. "You get started," he said, "and I'll dry the dishes."

"Okay," she replied, as she opened the back door. "I'll throw out this dishwater, but I'm not going to look up the hill right now!"

Lucius laughed, and nodded agreement. "I sure can wait until milking time to see them again!"

Almarine sat down and opened the journal. She looked at the heading on the page in front of her and grinned. "The journal fell open at the account I wrote about the day Sissy Warfield called me a witch! I thought she was just jealous because I make a little money with my witch hazel remedies, but after this morning, well..."

Lucius laughed. "Read the account about that. It might help get our brains squared up a bit with reality."

Almarine nodded agreement, "Good idea. Then I'll read the one we wrote after the landslide killed them, and see if we need to add anything before we tackle writing what we saw this morning."

As Almarine began to read the entry *The Day I Was Called a Witch* aloud, she was glad it was there. That memory gave her a sense of normalcy.

### Journal Entry — The Day I Was Called a Witch

"Preacher Hugh Darrow died last year, the day after Thanksgiving. It was bitter cold. Brother Josh Hammell, one of our deacons, agreed to preach the funeral on Saturday at noon. Lucius went over to help dig the grave, and I rode over later to the graveyard in the Warfields' wagon. I had cut witch hazel branches, loaded with flowers and seeds, and made a big pretty spray.

This photo of witch hazel courtesy Dr. David Kinder, dubbed the Mad Scientist by one of his students, at Ohio Northern University.

Logo from his Website.

"I could tell Sissy Warfield looked down on my spray even before she remarked that she'd never considered using witch hazel because she thought it was a bewitched plant. Why else, she opined, was it called a "witching stick?"

"I knew she was talking about dowsers using it. Seth Warfield knew that Lucius had brought a dowser from Bryson City when he and Fonzie were trying to find copper, and tried to explain to his wife. But Sissy was bent on being perverse.

" 'I can abide the gold leaves, but them tight clusters of so-called flowers look like pizen spiders.' "

"Sissy had made two lopsided cedar wreaths and put two big black bows on both of them.

"If I had not been on my way to pay my last respects to a man I pitied, I might not have been able to hold my tongue. Preacher Darrow and his wife had no children, and he had outlived all his kinfolk.

"By the time we got to the graveyard, it was spitting snow, and there wasn't much of a crowd. The men who had dug the grave had a fire going at the foot of the grave, and everybody was huddled around it. There were several wreaths and sprays on the grave, and all of them were green cedar or holly. Some had colored ribbons and flowers cut out of wood, or made with corn shucks, and dyed red with elderberries."

### A Few Moments of Reflection

Almarine stopped reading and took a sip of water from the dipper Lucius had placed on the table. She felt less tense and was pleased to see a grin tugging at the corners of Lucius' mouth.

"Don't say it again," she commanded.

Lucius let the grin transform his face, and asked in mock innocence, "Say what again?"

"You know very well what I mean!" Almarine retorted. "You always say I describe things like people can't remember. But I want to remind you that I expect this journal to be read long after we're gone, and the way things change, nobody will know what things were like in our day."

Lucius patted her hand. "You're right, just as always. I forget how much things have changed since I was a boy. Please finish reading about Sissy. Remembering that day has lifted my spirits considerably."

### Continuation of — The Day I Was Called a Witch

"Sissy placed her lopsided wreaths in the center of the grave, one on each side of the peak and almost took a bow.

"I thought about the time Preacher Darrow had come to our house suffering awful with poison ivy itch all over both legs, and got relief with my witch hazel remedy. That made it seem fitting to place my spray at the foot of his grave.

"Brother Hammell asked one of the boys to put a couple of logs on the fire and we'd get started. He explained that because it was so cold, his wife would not be playing the dulcimer, but she would lead the singing.

"He asked us to recite the Lord's Prayer. When we raised our heads, Mrs. Hammell reminded us that *Bound for the Promised Land* had been Preacher Darrow's favorite song, and led us through it at a spirited pace.

"Brother Hammell held his Bible toward the sky and said, 'Preacher Darrow loved this song. He's gone to the promised land! Listen to the words again — *"Sickness and sorrow, pain and death, are felt and feared no more."* And...'

"A cracking pop from the fire stopped him. I knew instantly that the seed pods on my witch hazel spray had exploded, because they always do when they get hot enough, and I said so in a loud voice. The sound was much sharper on that still hilltop than when they explode in the witch hazel patch. Mrs. Bradshaw screamed that the Devil was trying to keep Preacher Darrow from getting into the promised land!

"I had put a lot of big clusters of seed pods into the spray, and all of them were getting hot. I started over to move it but, before I got there some of the seeds hit Sissy Warfield.

"She let her eyes roll back in her head, then bowed her head and started praying in a shrill voice, 'O Lord, deliver us from the witch that walks among us. Thou knowest who she is. I know who she is, and I will do my duty.'

"She raised her head, grabbed my spray and threw it in the fire! More seeds exploded. People realized what was happening and began to laugh and jump in mock horror.

"Sissy was furious, but outnumbered. Brother Hammell knew about Preacher Darrow's bout with poison ivy, and told that story. He said that what happened was fitting because the witch hazel bush is one of God great healing and helping bushes and had given him comfort while he lived, and "sung" a song for him as he went to the Promised Land.

"Then Brother Hammell prayed a little. Some of the men put out the fire, and it was over. Nobody left the graveyard with a really sad heart. My spray was burned, but I vowed to always take witch hazel sprays to his grave at decoration time.

"After we got home, Lucius accused me of putting the spray near the fire on purpose. At first he said he thought I had done it, because everybody was standing so close they would have to notice it. After the seeds popped, he said he knew I had put it there so the seeds would get hot, pop, and some would hit Sissy Warfield.

"Truthfully, I cannot deny the first accusation, but I can deny the second one — but only because I did not think of it!

"I'll end this account with a drawing of how my spray probably looked to Sissy Warfield that day."

Almarine held the journal over so Lucius could see her handiwork again. "What do you think?

Lucius chucked. "Yep, that's just about the way I remember your spray looked that day!"

Almarine wanted to postpone reading what they had written after the landslide, but it had to be done. The title of the entry — *The End of Our Copper Mine — July 4, 1885* — brought it all back. She lifted the corner of her apron and wiped her eyes. Lucius patted her shoulder. After a few moments of silence, she read the next entry in their journal.

### The End of Our Copper Mine — July 4, 1885

"We were having a square dance to celebrate the first week of mining copper in our mine. About 50 people had come in spite of the preachers telling everybody that dancing is a sin.

"Uncle John Hall was playing the fiddle, and doing the calling. Willie Paul Jenkins was helping with the banjo. Without any warning, a terrible landslide came down the mountain just above the entrance to our copper mine. It sealed the entrance with tons of rock and dirt, buried five people alive under it, and hurt a dozen or more.

"Uncle John, Melvin and Joleen Rister, Ennis Cartwell and Louise Wiggins were the ones buried alive. People came from all over Swain and Macon counties with shovels, picks, hoes, and anything else that would break rocks and move dirt.

"Several preachers came to help. Some dug and prayed. Preacher Flaughtery kept telling Lucius that if he'd repent about dancing, God might show mercy and let them get to the bodies. And, he kept yelling, 'Dancing will land you and your wife in Hell.'

"Lucius yelled back, 'I'm not going to be a hypocrite and pretend I believe dancing is a sin. If dancing is a sin, why do you dance all around the church and shout 'Whoopee' while you're preaching?'

"Preacher Sutton, one of the Baptist preachers, stepped in between Lucius and Preacher Flaughtery and said the time had come to stop talking and digging, and hold a funeral. He said everybody should be there the next morning at ten o'clock.

"More than a hundred people came to the funeral. Most faced it as a hardship of life among the hills, and we comforted each other with the sweetness of memories. Most everybody who was able pitched in and helped move five big rocks in a row to mark the graves. Willie Paul Jenkins' brother, Joshua, had chiseled the names into the rocks.

"We moved here to Hazel Creek with great dreams after my brother, Jacob Alfonse "Fonzie" Hall, discovered copper in 1883 on land that our father, Jesse Hall, owns. He has promised to transfer his grant for 236 acres from the State of North Carolina to us, but has not done that yet.

"The best place to get to the copper is now a graveyard. There is no money to find another place to get to the copper.

"For now, Lucius will cut timber and farm. I, Almarine, will go back to making witch hazel remedies to sell."

Almarine finished reading the entry about the end of their copper mine and looked up. Lucius got up and put more wood in the stove, and brought another dipper of water to the table. "Here, take a sip."

"Thanks. Reading does make my throat dry."

### Coming to Terms With the Present

Lucius returned the dipper to the water bucket and sat down with a sigh, and his voice trembled slightly. "Hearing it brought it all back. We don't need to add anything about the landslide. But do you know what I think, Almarine?"

She shook her head. "No, tell me."

"What we saw this morning was a gift from God, and I will not question it. We will never be able to explain it, but the music, the voices, and the spirits will comfort us to the end of our days if we accept it with humility. You know I'm not big on parading around talking religion, but that's the terms

I've come to about what we saw up there. What do you think?" he asked expectantly.

Her face clouded, and she took a few moments to consider what he had said. She felt empty, as if the good angel of intelligence had fled her mind and left only a washtub full of emotions. She rubbed some of them — Bible verses, memories of ghost tales, fear, and curiosity — across the washboard, but got no better explanation of their strange vision.

Taking Lucius' hands in hers, she spoke in a firm, quiet voice, "I guess you're right, and if we can keep steady on that thinking, we won't let fear ride through us like a wild unbridled horse. I don't understand any of it, because it doesn't fit anything I've seen or been told about living and dying. All we can do for now is accept it and hope. Let's write down what we saw this morning."

This is what they wrote in their journal.

### October 10, 1885 — We Saw Ghosts

"This morning at daybreak we were at the milk gap when we heard a fiddle playing over at the copper mine. We looked and saw Uncle John with his fiddle. We heard him play and call the square dance just like he did just before the landslide. We saw Melvin and Joleen Rister, Ennis Cartwell and Louise Wiggins go through several sets.

"The sun was coming up, and we saw them as plain as day. Their bodies looked kind of like gossamer material at times, but they were solid enough for us to recognize them. They danced on top of the landslide that buried them on July 4, 1885, around the big boulders we used as headstones.

"We know they are dead, but we know we saw them. Until today we thought there was only one ghost, the Holy Ghost. Now we know there are at least five ghosts, because we don't know what else to call them.

"We were scared out of our wits most of the time. But we are no longer scared, because we have decided God gave us this marvelous experience to comfort us in our grief for those whose lives were snuffed out in the twinkling of an eye."

Almarine dropped her pencil in the holder, and asked, "Don't you want to draw something this time to mark the end of this entry? It's the most amazing thing that's ever happened to us."

Lucius reached for a sharp pencil, and said, "I think so. I'll draw what came into my head that made me tell you that I think what we saw up there this morning is a gift from God Almighty to comfort us."

Almarine pushed the journal in front of him. When he had finished this sketch he explained, "God sent a message down to our eyes and ears that the ones He took are dancing in the great beyond."

### After the Ghosts Danced

Almarine's father, Jesse Hall, kept his promise and deeded several hundred acres of land to Lucius Kinsland. This was the practice in that day and time — to deed the land to the husband, and not the wife, even though she was his daughter.

Lucius and Almarine did tell their family and friends that they had seen the ghosts dancing at the mine. True to Lucius' prediction, his mother had a glorious time telling them, "I told you there were ghosts."

Most of the people took their story with a grain of salt, but a few declared they believed them, and some professed seeing ghosts dancing at the mine.

Some of the local preachers told them they were in the grip of the devil, and to repent. They did not recant or repent.

Lucius and Almarine saw the ghosts of Uncle John and the other four who were killed in the landslide several times before they moved from Hazel Creek.

On two occasions, they saw them when they were together, and each of them saw them several times when they were alone around the mine.

### Efforts to Reopen the Mine

Lucius and Almarine farmed the land to produce most of their food, and raised cattle and hogs.

Lucius took jobs as a carpenter and blacksmith in various towns, and this meant he stayed away from home for long periods of time. Neither he nor Almarine like this arrangement, but tolerated it with the hope of reopening the mine.

Almarine dubbed herself "The Witch of Hazel Creek," and brewed remedies from the witch hazel bushes.

She sold them to people in the community, and Lucius sold them to people in the towns where he had jobs.

### The Fate of the Hazel Creek Copper Mine

In 1887, Lucius was approached by a New York mineral developer, W.S. Adams, about selling his land. By this time, he and Almarine had accepted the fact they would never be financially able to reopen a mine. They sold the land to Adams and moved to Bryson City, North Carolina, and lived there until they died.

Adams also bought land from several other people, including Jesse Hall, Almarine's father. When he began to build roads to get to his mining site, about a dozen property owners who held land grants from the State of North Carolina began to dispute his title. After futile efforts in the courts until 1899, he defied his challengers and sunk two mine shafts.

Adams had to halt operations because of the legal dispute over his ownership of the land had escalated. He died in 1910, with the dispute still in litigation. His heirs prevailed sufficiently to sink new shafts in 1942, but the operation also failed.

In 1943 the Tennessee Valley Authority (TVA) acquired 44,000 acres of land from Swain County, and this included the Hazel Creek community. All the public roads were closed.

TVA did not use this land, and it became part of the Great Smoky Mountains National Park.

### Hazel Creek in 2002

Hazel Creek still flows, and its banks are still adorned with the witch hazel bushes that gave the creek its name.

Photograph courtesy Fred Douglas Bean

Because all the public roads have remained closed since 1943 there are two ways to get to the area that was once Hazel Creek community — hiking and by boat.

For those who do not own a boat, there is a marina at Fontana Village that offers boat service across the lake.

Nature is slowly but surely obliterating all traces of the inhabitants. Only a few traces of the homes and farm buildings remain.

Descendants of Hazel Creek residents are preserving several cemeteries, and decorate the graves with flowers.

Some of the copper mines are still surrounded by a barren area, with no vegetation, and slag mounds. When mining was going on, there were no laws to protect the environment, so the operators just walked away and left the open wounds.

The National Park Service has posted signs warning of the dangers of going close to the mines. Only ghosts can enter them with safety!

### Do Ghosts Still Dance on Hazel Creek?

If you are on Hazel Creek and hear a sound that seems out of place — listen — and look around! You may see Uncle John and/or the square dancers!

Jb Original

## Author's Note

Lucius Harvey Kinsland learned before his death that his father was John Stallcup, and he corrected his surname to Stallcup. He and Maude Almarine Elizabeth Hall are my paternal great-grandparents.

I first heard the story about ghosts dancing on Hazel Creek the summer before I started to school. My grandmother, Mary Birchfield Stallcup, had taken me with her to visit her sister, Josie Stallcup, who was also her sister-in-law because they had married two of Lucius' and Almarine's sons. Their sister, Laura, had also married one of their sons.

We sat in rockers on the front porch, and I was expected to be quiet and play with my string puzzle while they talked. Having been born with an overactive curiosity, I soaked up what adults said like a dry sponge.

I'd learned that the best parts came when they were being careful about what they said in front of me. I could tell when they were being careful by the way they looked in my direction. But that hurdle was a breeze to overcome — I just went to "sleep" and the censoring stopped!

## Chapter 5
## An Enigma — Bells Hanging in Trees

Alla Trent, Robin Kelly and I were hiking in Cocke County, Tennessee, in October 1996. We were searching for the homesite where John and Mary Jane Ramsey had lived in 1919. Their three-year-old son, Abe Carroll Ramsey, disappeared and has never been found.

At that time I was researching the story, and it was subsequently published in the book *Unsolved Disappearances in the Great Smoky Mountains*. We never did find the exact site, but we did encounter an enigma of bells hanging in trees, and solved it!

Alla spotted a bell hanging in a tree over what appeared to be a birdhouse. "Wonder if they call the birds with that bell?"

We laughed, and thought no more about it until we saw another bell hanging in a tree over a box made of rough lumber.

"That's not a birdhouse," Robin declared.

"Wonder if this one is to call the bears or scare them away? It's too far out in the woods to be some farmer's dinner bell."

We agreed, and decided to ask the next person we saw for an explanation. Later in the afternoon, we met a middle-aged man and woman on the trail and stopped to chat. Alla waited until we'd had a pleasant exchange, then asked whether either of them knew why so many people way out in the woods hung bells in trees.

They burst into robust laughter, and the woman, who had introduced herself as Tina Garrett, asked if we had rung any of the bells.

Alla replied, "Yes, I rang the second bell we saw, but nothing happened."

"Or so you think!" Jim Garrett exclaimed. "If you go back, there may be a drink of moonshine waiting!"

We were intrigued. Between the Garretts, subsequent research and conversations with lots of other people, we learned that hanging a bell in a tree is a unique way to sell moonshine, a sour mash whiskey that is the stuff of legends.

### Ring the Bell to Order Moonshine

Moonshine is a cash crop, albeit illegal. When certain moonshiners are ready to sell, they put out a press release via word of mouth among the trusted locals. Current prices are included in it.

Moonshiners use this unique marketing method to ensure that there is never any face-to-face contact between supplier and customer. The seller hangs a bell in a tree and installs a simple receptacle. People who want a drink, or a jar of moonshine, ring the bell, leave the correct amount of money and then stroll out of sight for a few minutes. No change is given, because money carries fingerprints.

The stroll gives the moonshiner an opportunity to scrutinize the customer. If he or she passes muster, the order will be filled. The customer is expected to consume the delight swiftly, or grab the bag with one or more jars in it, and move on without delay.

This is standard operating procedure because selling moonshine is a high-risk, illegal business that makes every customer a potential threat.

The location of the moonshine still is a carefully-guarded secret, far from the bell tree. Only a small supply is kept nearby. We did not determine for certain where the storage area for the bell tree where we rang the bell was, but we had strong suspicions that a shed near the path was used.

Ever since George Washington placed a tax on all whiskey in 1794, the government has been in the business of regulating the making and selling of whiskey in order to collect taxes on it.

The government's determination to collect taxes, and the moonshiners' determination to not pay them, is an ongoing battle. Moonshining is as much of an economic issue as a moral one.

And that is why the making of moonshine has generally died out. Moonshiners cannot sell whiskey as cheaply as the giants who make it legally, although they vow that the legal product is inferior to *real good 'shine*. The mountains are no longer as safe a place to hide a still as they were during the moonshine heyday years — the 1850s to the 1930s. Better roads and communications make it very easy to get caught.

So, if you have a hankering for moonshine, expect to pay a premium price.

Prohibition, according to one moonshiner I interviewed, was the best thing the government had ever done for the economy of the Great Smoky Mountains. "People," he said, "have drunk whiskey probably since Adam and Eve were thrown out of the Garden of Eden, and I believe they will until Gabriel blows his trumpet. We hated to see Prohibition end because our income gradually dried up. And so did a lot of the thrills and excitement of getting it to our customers by outrunning the law in our "souped-up" cars."

Moonshining was never as glamorous as portrayed in the movie *Thunder Road,* or as fatal as the sad story told in *The Ballad of Thunder Road*. Moonshine runners can take much of the credit for starting stock car racing in the South. After the demand for their 'shine dried up, they got the idea of racing against each other in one place for a paying audience, and created a new, very profitable sport.

Horace Kephart told it like it really was in his book *Our Southern Highlanders*, in the chapter "Ways That Are Dark."

### We Rang the Bell for Moonshine

We went back to the closest tree with a bell hanging in it, put $5 in the slot, rang the bell, and took a short stroll. Our order was not filled.

Later that afternoon, we saw the Garretts at a roadside rest stop, and told them we had tried to make a buy. They laughed, and told us that they had made a buy one day, but felt they'd been had. They recognized the stuff they got as Kessler whiskey — and it is sold in stores!

So, be warned! If you chance upon a bell in a tree it may belong to a moonshiner peddling real 'shine, or be a unique tourist trap!

## Chapter 6
## The Sinks — A Place of Myth and Mystery

The Sinks is an area of waterfalls, rapids and deep pools in the Little River, about twelve miles west of the Sugarlands Visitor Center, going toward Townsend, Tennessee, in Great Smoky Mountains National Park. It is visible from Little River Road, and there is a small parking area.

I'd heard an intriguing tale that early in the 20th century, a logging train derailed into the Sinks and has never been found. I had to see the site of this unsolved mystery.

This is a picture of the bridge on Little River Road, and part of the Sinks, on a tranquil fall day.

Photo courtesy of Richard Weisser and smokyphotos.com

Cas Walker, a local self-made multimillionaire, politician, writer, and colorful entertainer, who gave Dolly Parton her first break into the music industry, was born near the Sinks in 1902, and lived in the Smokies until his death in 1998.

Walker described it as a place of great beauty and great terror. And after I visited the Sinks several times, and heard stories about it, this is an apt description.

### Running the Little River

Little River Road runs beside Little River for a couple of miles before you get to the Sinks. This is a good place for tubers, but everyone should get out of the river at the first glimpse of the Sinks bridge because the turbulent, swirling water makes it a hazardous place. The rocks are treacherous, and diving from them is like Russian roulette.

Even very experienced and well equipped whitewater veterans find the Sinks a real challenge.

Scott Gravatt in the Sinks (Photograph by Bob Maxey - 4/26/00)
http://www.blueridgevoyageurs.org

Despite the hazards, too many people play in and around the Sinks. And people die here every year. A contributing factor may be the sites on the World Wide Web, and in tourist brochures that tout the Sinks as "the deepest swimmin' hole in the Smokies," without a single word of warning.

### My First Visit to the Sinks

My first glimpse of the Sinks was on a dismal, clouded morning. I had driven there alone, and the parking lot was empty. The water in Little River was high that day. It roared in wild and undisturbed dominion over the channel through the rocks.

The huge old overhanging trees were dripping, and crows were cawing from their high roosts. A few soft-eyed, shy deer peeping from beneath the branches kept the scene from being straight out of Edgar Allan Poe. I watched for a few minutes, then exited the car and began snapping pictures.

### Dafne

From the bridge, I spotted an inner tube swirling madly in the maelstrom. After a few minutes, a high splash slammed it up on to the rocks. I was so intent on getting it into focus that I was startled to hear a voice exclaim, "That was awesome, and I got the whole thing on video!"

I whirled around and was quite relieved to see that the voice belonged to a pretty young woman in backpacking gear. She smiled. "Sorry, if I scared you. The water is roaring like a lion today. I should have called out."

"It's okay," I recall saying. "I'm glad you're here. This place is kind of spooky today."

Her smile vanished. She looked down at the fury below, and asked in a serious tone, "Have you ever seen the spirit of someone who died — a ghost?"

Intuition told me there was more to her question than small talk. I looked at her inquiringly, and replied with a semi-apologetic air, "No, not yet. Have you?"

She took a deep breath, glanced at me, then riveted her eyes on the roiling water below the bridge. Her reaction gave me immediate confirmation that my intuition was correct. I kept silent, but watched the changing expression that lit, then shadowed, her intent young face.

After a time, she looked at me and said with a note of tender sadness, "I came to see the spirit of a friend who drowned here. And I saw him just before you came." She lowered her head, and tears spilled onto her flushed cheeks.

I spoke as gently and sincerely as I could. "It appears it was a joyful experience for you."

"It was," she said. "Do you believe me?"

"Of course!" I told her, then added, "You look like you have your head screwed on straight."

She seemed relieved and her tears stopped. "It was an incredible experience. It seemed natural, not weird."

"Please tell me about your friend."

"I'd like to, if you have the time," she said, then added with an impish grin, "Maybe he'll join us. Then you can tell the next person who asks you if you've ever seen a ghost that you have!"

This was a strange, novel experience, and I was happy to see that the van that arrived at that moment slowed but kept going. I laughed, "If he does join us, I shall consider that substantial proof that ghosts exist!"

She smiled, and seemed to will herself to be composed. "His name is Michael. Mike to our whitewater cronies, but always Michael to me. We loved the sport. I want to be good at it, but Michael wanted to be the best." She pulled a small notebook from her jacket pocket. "I'm making a written record about him, and had just described what happened today before you arrived. Writing makes me organize my thoughts. Rather than tell you about him, may I read a little of what I've written?"

"Please do."

"Michael Mulholland had a dogged power of continuity that would have carried him to the highest pinnacle of achievement, and won him worldwide fame, but for a catastrophe here in the Sinks. He capsized and drowned. In an instant he, and all his dreams, were gone. Simple as that. I was left to live with an unconquerable remorse because I did not do more to stop him from making that fatal run.

"Today I came to the Sinks, confident that I would be able to contact his spirit. And I did. No one may believe me, and maybe it's my imagination, but I saw Michael. His image was on the bank, just below the spot where he went under. He smiled and waved. He must be alive in another dimension."

I waited a few moments, but she had finished reading and looked at me for a response. "I am sorry you lost Michael, but I'm sure from your description of him that you could not have stopped him. When you see him again, ask him. That will help you conquer your remorse."

"Good idea," she said in a preoccupied tone. "I guess he's not going to show while we're talking."

"Meeting you and hearing your story has been great," I replied. "And I would enjoy meeting Michael."

The young woman, whose name I did not yet know, giggled. "I think you really believe me, but then again you may be just humoring me because you fear you've encountered a nut, and she's standing between you and your car!"

I extended my hand with a warm smile and said, "I don't think you're a nut. I'm Juanitta Baldwin, and I live in Kodak

— that's a place about 35 miles down the road. I came here to make pictures for a book I'm writing, and this conversation with you will make a great story!"

"Good Lord!" she exclaimed with a half smile. "You're really serious?"

"I am," I said with a firm shake of my head.

There was a slight pause, and then she said with a happy sigh, "I'll tell you my real name and where I'm from, but please don't use it in your story. My father is a man of the cloth, and he would not be happy for the world to know his only daughter is into ghosts."

"No problem," I assured her. "I respect that, and protect my sources. What if I call you Daphne in the story?"

"Okay. I like that name, but spell it — D-a-f-n-e. I love words that are spelled as they sound."

The sun banished the mist. Dafne and I sat down on the bank and enjoyed a cup of coffee from my thermos, some of her high-energy trail mix.

After an exhilarating chat, we said goodbye. Every trip to the Smokies is an adventure, but this encounter with Dafne at the Sinks was one of the richest. We have become friends, but I am still waiting to meet Michael!

### Train in the Sinks?

The major reason I had gone to the Sinks was a tale I'd heard that in the early 20th century a logging train had plunged into the Sinks, and was never been found because the water was so deep that no one could reach the bottom.

Logging in the Great Smoky Mountains was a major industry in the late 19th and early 20th centuries. To get the logs out, miles and miles of railroad were built all over the Smokies. Little River Road follows the route of a railroad.

That day, looking at the hydraulic rapids above the bridge, which are huge waves caused by the steep drops in the river bed, I could believe that they could swallow a train as easily the whale swallowed Jonah. But I had grave doubts about that it could have stayed out of site, and decided to check further.

I checked the "train in the Sinks story" at the Little River Railroad and Lumber Company Museum in Townsend, Tennessee. They have no record to substantiate this intriguing tale, but there is a plethora of interesting history about trains and logging.

The museum is at the west entrance to the Great Smoky Mountains National Park. Highway access is from Interstate 40 or Interstate 75.

Website: http://www.littleriverrailroad.org/museum.

## Chapter 7
## Lone Grave Marker —
## A Story About the White Caps and Blue Bills

### Preface

I had never heard of White Caps and Blue Bills until I moved to Tennessee. Hence I am writing this preface, because without some background about who they were and what they did, many readers would find this story impossible to believe.

### How I Heard This Story

Lone graves, with or without markers, always intrigue me. Who, I wonder, reached the end of their journey on Earth at that spot. And why? This story is the result of my asking questions about a lone marker that I and some friends chanced upon in a deep hollow in the hills of Tennessee in January 1999.

It is a hollow where marijuana is the current cash crop, and dark secrets are quietly kept. The skill to banish inquisitive strangers is passed down from generation to generation.

This hollow was the scene of many crimes by the White Cap Society, a secret society similar to the Ku Klux Klan, that terrorized Sevier County, and parts of surrounding counties, from the late 19th century to about 1910.

The Society was formed by a group of men who believed that the courts in Sevier County and the state of Tennessee were not punishing evildoers, and took matters into their own hands. They took an oath, under penalty of severe punishment, even death, not to reveal anything about any White Cap, the White Caps Society or anything that they did, and to stand by each other regardless of the circumstances. They identified each other by slight hand signals.

Passing the right hand over the right cheek indicated, "I'm a White Cap." Passing the left hand over the left cheek answered, "So am I."

Their modus operandi was to notify people they deemed to be immoral, usually in writing, to change their behavior or leave the community within a certain time or they would be whipped with hickory switches.

After a short time even those who could not read understood what a batch of switches meant.

If the people did not obey, a gang of men shrouded in white, with only slits for the eyes and mouth cut out, appeared in the dead of night to punish without mercy.

The white covering, combined with the victim's terror, made it almost impossible to identify a White Cap.

There are no known reliable statistics, but scores of people were whipped into submission or driven from their homes, beaten or shot to death. The White Caps were so successful in intimidating the community that gradually they became bold enough to carry out their edicts in broad daylight.

### Blue Bills Organized to Combat the White Caps

The terror became so widespread that a group of men formed an organization called the Blue Bills to combat the White Caps.

The Blue Bills had widespread support from the residents of Sevier County, but most were afraid to take a public stand. But this silent support made it possible for them to get information about the White Cap membership, and were able to infiltrate their organization and know in advance what they planned to do.

Armed with this information, they would follow the White Caps to the appointed place and hide to surprise them in action and shoot them down. The White Caps always shot back. There were many battles, and much loss of life on both sides.

The sheriff and the courts seemed powerless to stop the White Caps. In the rare instances when a case when to court, the offenders were always set free because the White Caps controlled the juries by packing them with their members.

The Blue Bills, and many citizens, began an intense lobby in the Tennessee Legislature to pass a bill to outlaw the White Caps. But it took the White Caps' execution of Laura and William Whaley to get action.

The motive for these murders was money, not morals. The couple were murdered in the dead of night, and the White Caps did not know there was an adult woman in bed in another room. The woman heard Laura Whaley beg for the life of her baby daughter, and they allowed her to put the child in bed. She put the child in bed with the woman, who heard everything the White Caps said and did.

The next day the woman went for help, and told how the Whaleys had begged for their lives, but had been shot in cold blood. More than five hundred people viewed the Whaleys, prostrate in pools of blood on the floor of their humble cabin, and heard the piteous cries of the baby that had been orphaned.

### The Beginning of the End for the White Caps

The brutal Whaley murders ignited the smoldering fire of sentiment against the White Caps. People, who had not dared express their outrage at the White Caps, began to talk.

Nobody was safe. The realization sunk in that the White Caps no longer whipped those they deemed to be immoral, but everybody they could not control for their own ends. Talk became epidemic. People began to watch anyone suspected of being a White Cap and take what action they could, and they gave strong support to the Blue Bills.

The officers of the law were pressured to find the men who had murdered the Whaleys, and arrest them. The Tennessee Legislature met on the first Monday in January 1898, only a few days after the Whaley murders. People went to Nashville and demanded legislation to outlaw the White Caps. On March 24, 1898, the governor signed the anti-White Cap bill into law.

Two White Caps, Pleas Wynn and Catlett Tipton, were charged with the murder of the Whaleys under the new anti-White Cap law.

They were tried, convicted and sentenced to die by public hanging. On July 5, 1899, they were hanged in front of the Sevier County Courthouse in Sevierville. More than three thousand people watched.

Photograph courtesy George Self

The families of both men were there. Wynn was baptized about an hour before he was taken to the hanging platform.

During their trial, Wynn and Tipton had testified that White Cap Bob Catlett had paid them $25 each to murder the Whaleys.

Bob Catlett was charged, but his case was continued until after Wynn and Tipton were hanged. Subsequently it was continued from one court to another. Most records state that his lawyers "just wore it out in court" until the charges were dropped.

After Wynn and Tipton were hanged, the White Caps Society began to disintegrate. It ceased to exist as an organized force of terror about 1910.

In 2002, there are no gallows in front of the Sevier County courthouse, but it looks about the same as it did when Wynn and Tipton were hanged. It had been completed in 1896.

The front is now flanked on the left by a memorial honoring military veterans, and on the right by a statue of Dolly Parton, Sevier County's most famous daughter, strumming her guitar.

Sevier County Courthouse
Photograph courtesy Jim Long

### Author's Note

Before I decided to include the story about the White Caps and Blue Bills in this book, I researched the White Caps Society and the Blue Bills. There are many reliable records in the Sevier County Library. Many people shared oral history.

A book by Cas Walker, a local poor boy who became a millionaire, *The White Caps of Sevier County* was very informative. It was published in 1937, and is still in print.

I have no probative evidence that the story is accurate in all details, but this crime fits their modus operandi and I could not exclude it.

## The Lone Grave Marker

This is a photograph I made of the lone grave marker I wanted to know more about.

The marker is a mixture of concrete and gravel. The inscription — KESSLER SOME TiMES DEAD IS BETTER — was scratched into the concrete while it was soft.

The marker is a rectangle and we could tell it had been poured in a frame. There were no signs of the frame, so we concluded that it had either been removed or the marker was poured at another site and moved to its present location.

The property where we saw the marker was for sale, so this opened the door for questions. The owners said that they had inherited the property from a distant relative about twenty years before, had never been on all of it, and did not know about the marker. They made inquiries, but did not come up with any information.

I lost interest as a potential land buyer, but not in the marker. It was logged into my computer in the "Things to Check When and If I Ever Get Around to It" list.

I court serendipity this way, and got around to it gradually over the next two years.

### How the Story Developed

My friends and I went back to the site, made a lot of pictures, and examined the marker very carefully.

I researched the history of concrete on the World Wide Web, and found that experts can establish the approximate age of concrete. We chipped off a small piece and asked a concrete contractor about the age of the material. He said it looked to be between 50 and 60 years old.

I got a plat of the area, and a list of the people who own property that joins the property where the marker is located, from the Sevier County Courthouse. I phoned and/or wrote all the property owners. Zilch — no one knew about "Kessler."

The Smoky Mountain Historical Society allowed me to post this inquiry in the Spring 1999 issue of their Journal:

*"Mystery Marker: I am attempting to identify the origin of what appears to be a grave marker on a wooded lot in Sevier County. The full inscription reads: 'KESSLER SOME TiMES DEAD IS BETTER.' No one living near this lot acknowledges knowing anything about it. Any information on this name, etc. will be appreciated."* Information on how to contact me was included below the post.

Several people did contact me. One person suggested I check the records for the World War II Camp Crossville in Crossville, Tennessee, where German prisoners of war were held from 1942-1945. There were lots of rumors that despite the government's denial, several prisoners had escaped and were never captured. The caller said that after all this time I might be able to get the records under the Freedom of Information Act.

This was fascinating stuff. I did not know prisoners of war had ever been confined in the United States. During my research, I learned a lot about prisoners of war and Camp Crossville, but found no evidence to link an escaped prisoner to this marker, but lots of possibilities for future stories.

From January 1999 to June 2000, as time and circumstance permitted, I and other people who had become interested in this mystery marker checked all the available records at the Sevier County Library, at the Lawson McGhee Library in Knoxville, and on the World Wide Web. The name "Kessler" was not found in Sevier County.

But the word went out, and a woman offered to tell me what she knew about the marker, on the condition of absolute anonymity. With anonymity assured, she told me the story that follows, which I have titled "A White Cap Crime." It is told from the prospective of a granddaughter whose grandfather was a White Cap.

### A White Cap Crime

A year before he died, my grandfather told my grandmother that he poured two cement markers to ease his conscience for a deed he had done when he was wild and sinful.

The deed was done in 1907, but he did not pour the markers until about 1939. He carved the words "KESSLER SOME TiMES DEAD IS BETTER" on both of them with his pocket knife before the cement dried too hard. He always dotted his "i" even when printing in capital letters. When I saw this in the inquiries about it, I was sure it is the marker he made.

   Grandpa was born in Sevier County and lived here most of his life. His family farmed, raised cattle, and trapped foxes to sell the furs. They were respectable, law-abiding people, and members of the Holy Rollers — that's what the Baptists called the Holiness church people. Socially, the Holy Rollers were on a lower rung than Baptists or Methodists. And in his day, these were the major religions in Sevier County.

Grandpa went to the altar and got "saved" when he was twelve. He was taught that chewing "terbacker," drinking spirits, dancing, lusting after women, cock fighting, telling lies, stealing, and gambling were terrible sins. His mother never committed these sins, but his father dabbled in all of them except lying.

When he was 17 Grandpa got a job cutting timber with the Little River Lumber Company. The same company owned the Little River Railroad Company, and sometimes he helped load the logs on the railroad cars that hauled them out of the mountains. Sometimes he rode atop a loaded railroad car to the sawmill.

The work was hard and the pay was good. He helped his folks a little but wasted a lot of money. Being away from home Grandpa began to backslide. First it was taking a few nips at a "blind tiger" — a bootlegger — and gambling.

A bunch of women moved into a cabin in a hollow where the log train passed, and the word went out that men with money could go there for a night of carousing. Before long, he was carousing with the best of them.

When Grandpa went home, he'd go to church with his family. The preacher would tick off the list of sins he'd committed, just like he'd been there and seen him commit them.

Then he'd hold his Bible over his head and shout, "There's a young man here who needs to confess! God be merciful to that backslider."

The first few months, grandpa would go to the altar and confess he'd been a-foolin' with women, and all the rest. By the time he was 18, he was a worldly backslider, and quit going to church. His father didn't say a whole lot, but his mother grieved over him.

### Grandpa Joined the White Caps

Grandpa's boss was a White Cap. White Caps tried to keep their membership a secret, but word got around. Once he'd heard his boss and two men talking about "being forced to shoot" an old man who had stood in their way of whipping his daughter who was not living up to their moral standards. The next day he heard who had been shot to death.

Nobody in Grandpa's family was either a White Cap or a Blue Bill. They never bothered anybody, and didn't want anybody sticking their nose in their business. Grandpa was glad he didn't have any sisters.

One Saturday night Grandpa had lost his week's wages in a card game. A fight had broken out, followed by some shooting, and one man was killed. Grandpa didn't have a gun, so he knew he hadn't killed the man. His boss came around and let Grandpa know that he had heard about what had happened on Saturday night, and offered to advance him some tobacco money.

Grandpa loved to chew tobacco to the day he died. He didn't want to be beholden to his boss, but facing a week without a chew, when it wasn't necessary to suffer like that, made the money irresistible.

On the next Friday, his boss climbed up on the log train he was to ride, and told him that if he'd do a "little rocking job" for him that night, he would not deduct the money he had advanced him from his pay. Grandpa agreed because he was afraid to say no.

That night he went to a house two miles from Sevierville. He did not know who lived there, or why his boss wanted them "rocked," because he knew better than to ask.

There was a thick boxwood bush in the front yard. He picked up rocks from the surrounding field and piled them behind it. After all the lights went out in the house, he began throwing rocks through the windows, as he had been told to do. The glass in those that were closed was shattered. He also hurled rocks through the open windows, but no one yelled like they had been struck.

Somebody stuck a shotgun out a front window and began firing. Grandpa was not hit. He ran around to the back, and sent a big rock flying through the only window on that side of the house. Figuring that the breaking glass would bring the shooter to the back, Grandpa raced down beside the house.

The shooter must have been out of bullets, because no more shots were fired, but he broke every closed window in the house before he left.

He had an old gun at home, but he took his wages for that week, went to Knoxville, and bought a brand new Winchester. It's still in the family.

On Monday mornings, the boss always got everybody together and gave out assignments for the week. He asked Grandpa to stay after the others left. Grandpa expected he wanted to know if he had "rocked" the house. When his boss shook his hand and told him what a good job he had done, Grandpa said he felt the hair on the back of his neck stand up.

He asked his boss how he knew what had happened. His boss told him he and a couple of his friends had hidden and watched. That "little job" had been to test his guts. Then his boss told him he'd have some more jobs for him, and maybe in time he could become "one of us."

Grandpa knew exactly what "one of us" meant. In the summer of 1907, he took the White Cap oath.

### The Horrible Deed

In July, his boss, now his White Cap leader, told him that he needed him to help him "whip out" a lewd woman who had tempted his son until he got her in the family way.

He said this woman was a 19-year-old strumpet from a family of low white trash. She had been warned, with a note and big bundle of hickory switches, to go back to Claiborne County where she'd come from. It had been a week, and she was still in Sevier County.

Grandpa had been in plenty of fights with men, and had heard about people being "whipped out," but he'd never seen it. He had a few thoughts about why only the woman, and not his son, was to blame, but that was just the way it was.

About midnight on the night that had been agreed upon, Grandpa rode a horse and met three men in the woods about a mile from the house where the woman was staying with her sister and brother-in-law.

The moon was bright in a cloudless sky. They were all on horseback, and everybody carried a rifle or a shotgun, or both. Two huge bundles of hickory switches were strapped across one of the horses. They slipped into their white robes, and galloped into the front yard of a small house in an open field close to the French Broad River.

Everybody jumped from their horses. Grandpa's job was to rein the horses, tie them to trees, and light three lanterns. The other men stormed onto the porch with switches in their hands. Grandpa took the lanterns up on the porch.

Grandpa's boss yelled, "Open this door. We've come to give that strollop Kessler what she's asked for." Nobody opened the door, so they kicked it open and went in. Grandpa and another man held the lanterns so they could look around.

The boss and the other man found two women huddled under a bed, and dragged them out. Both screamed and begged for mercy. They shoved the intended victim's sister onto a bed, and the pregnant victim was told to march into the yard. The brother-in-law was not at home. Grandpa learned later that his boss had known this beforehand.

The victim fell to the floor, like she had fainted. Two men grabbed her arms and dragged her onto the porch. Her sister begged them to stop. The boss silenced her with a severe blow over her head with a hickory switch.

Grandpa and another man held the lanterns while one man stood on each side and whipped her across the back until the blood pooled around her body. They turned her over, and the boss stepped back and told Grandpa and the other man, "Cut the other bundle of switches open, and don't stop until she quits breathing. Satan sent this she-devil to tempt and trap my son. She won't do it again in this world. Maybe in hell."

Grandpa said he felt like he was in hell by that time, and he could not obey his boss to finish beating that innocent woman to death. Knowing he'd be shot if he did not obey, he picked up his Winchester and fired a single shot into her head. In a few seconds, she was still. He felt her pulse, and nodded to the leader that she was dead.

The leader poked the dead woman's belly with the butt of his gun and yelled through the door to her sister, "We've killed the whore and her bastard. If you've got any more like her where you come from, and you bring them into our God-fearing community, next time we'll send you out with the slut."

There was no answer. The leader gave the signal and they got on their horses and rode away. By daylight, they were all back where they were expected to be, and their lips were sealed with the White Caps oath.

The next day the sheriff and his deputies went to the house where the woman had been murdered with a pack of bloodhounds. The trail went cold at the river, because the White Caps had ridden three miles in the river before they got out on the other side.

The law, and the community, were dead set against the White Caps by that time, but they were never caught. Grandpa said he was sick at the person he had become, and vowed to "get right with God." The next day he quit his job and went to Knoxville. He got a railroad job there, and stayed out of Sevier County for a long time except for short visits.

### Grandpa's Nightmares

Grandma said Grandpa had the most awful nightmares. Miss Kessler, the murdered woman, would rise up from that pool of blood and ask, "Why did you shoot me?" Why didn't you shoot the men and save me and my baby?"

He said he'd never forget the pattern in the dress she was wearing. He'd seen it lots of times, because it was made out of a feed sack, and every time he saw that pattern he'd break out in a cold sweat.

Back then, feed and flour came in cloth sacks that were imprinted with a design. The lettering that told what was in the sack would wash out. When the side and bottom seams were let out the purchaser had a yard or so of sewing fabric.

One summer, Grandma bought some seeds from a seed catalog for a plant she'd never seen. She planted two short rows in the front yard and all the plants bloomed just as promised. One day Grandpa pulled them up because they looked like the flowers in Miss Kessler's dress! Grandma never told him the name of the plant was Miss Wilmot's Ghost!

Grandpa's mother got sick, and his father sent word to him in Knoxville for him to come right away if he wanted to see her alive. As his daddy opened the kitchen door for him, he saw Miss Kessler. He backed up, sat down on the steps, and dropped his head in his hands. His daddy asked him what was wrong, but he couldn't answer.

After asking him a few more times, his daddy said he knew he was upset over his mother, and Grandpa let him think that. But what had happened was that when he had started into the house, his mother's feed sack apron was hanging on the kitchen door.

In the dim light he said it looked like the woman he shot because the pattern in the apron was the same pattern in the dress she'd had on.

Common sense told him it was an apron, but he also *knew* the dead woman had been there because he *saw* her.

To the day he died, grandma said he would turn pale, and sometimes get sick at his stomach, when he'd see that feed sack pattern,

We don't know what the pattern looked like.

**Author's Note:** This is a picture of a vintage feed sack apron pinned to a door to help visualize how the apron could resemble a person or a ghost.

## Grandpa's Life After He Left the White Caps

Grandpa's mother died. He said he thought about confessing to the law, but settled for confessing to God.

At the funeral he met a widow woman, with two little children, whose husband had been killed by the White Caps. He said she was a nice woman, but he did not marry her for love. He felt that if he married her and helped her raise those two children, he would be making some atonement for his part in Miss Kessler's murder.

They lived together for about ten years, and had five children. She died while giving birth to twin girls who died within a week. His children needed a mother, so in less than a month after he buried his first wife, he proposed marriage to another woman, with three children.

She had never been married, and all the children had different fathers. This is the kind of woman the White Caps would have beaten to death. More atonement, and a good deed for them both, he said. That wife is my grandmother. My mother was one of her illegitimate children.

They learned to love each other, and because she was the kind of woman she was, Grandpa felt free to talk with her about his wild and sinful life. He did not condemn her for having us three kids out of wedlock. She did not thump the Bible in his face, and he knew his secrets were safe with her.

## SOME TiMES DEAD IS BETTER

In the late 1930s Grandpa was working for a building contractor. One day he was pouring concrete about a mile from the house where he had shot Miss Kessler.

When the job concrete was finished, the couple who lived in the house came out and wrote their names and a short commemorative message. This gave Grandpa an idea.

That weekend he poured two rectangular blocks of cement, took his pocket knife and wrote the same words on both of them: KESSLER SOME TiMES DEAD IS BETTER. One was to mark the woman's grave, and the other was for her unborn baby.

Grandpa did not write Miss Kessler's first name because he did not know it. He said he may have heard her full name when her murder was being talked about, but if he had, he had forgotten it. But the name "Kessler" had been branded into his mind the night he helped murder her.

Grandpa said he had thought that night that shooting the woman was better than beating her to death. Anyway, that's why he put what he did on the markers — "SOME TiMES DEAD IS BETTER."

He did not know where Miss Kessler had been buried. Under cover of darkness, he took the markers into a remote, wooded area. He knelt and prayed for her forgiveness and for God's forgiveness, then placed one of the markers in the ground and covered it with leaves so it would not be noticed.

He heard some hounds top over the ridge above him, hot after a fox. He left real quick and drove a few miles down the road. He placed the other marker under some thick laurel bushes, and also covered it with leaves.

Grandpa told grandma that making those markers gave him a little peace, but he was tormented about the awful things he did as a White Cap, and especially being a murderer, until he died. Toward the end of his life, he stopped hunting and hired people to kill his hogs and beef. He died from lung cancer, a gift from his beloved "terbacker."

Grandpa often admonished us to shun evil, and would tell us in a sad tone, "The road I took in life runs right through the gates of Hell. My only hope is that the gates will open and let me into Heaven."

## Chapter 8
## Who Wrote on Judaculla Rock?

This is Judaculla Rock. It is on Caney Fork Road in Jackson County, North Carolina, and open to the public all year around, free of charge.

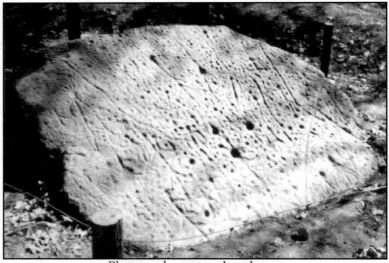
Photograph courtesy Jane Joyner

Judaculla stands alone in a small park. Detailed directions to it are at the end of this chapter.

It is a soapstone boulder, about 40 feet in circumference, covered with pictographic writings. As a writer, I salute the unknown author, or authors, for leaving this magnificent glimpse into the past, with an enviable degree of permanence.

But there the mystery begins. No one knows who wrote on Judaculla, when or what or they wrote. There is general agreement that the markings are not graffiti from an earlier time, but information that was important. However, despite extensive study by scholars and researchers, there is no agreement on what the writers are telling their readers.

James Mooney, author of *Myths of the Cherokee*, published in 1891, wrote that the story of "Jutaculla" is one of the finest and best known of the Cherokee legends. He explained that "Jutaculla" is a corruption of the name "Tsulkalu," a slant-eyed giant who is "great lord of the hunt." Since Mooney's day, "Jutaculla" has become "Judaculla," but the legend has not changed.

Judaculla had cleared about a hundred acres, on top of the ridge where Jackson, Haywood, and Transylvania counties converge, and farmed it. Judaculla had slanted eyes, could control the wind, rain, thunder and lightning, and was powerful enough to leap from one mountain to another.

The scratches on Judaculla Rock were made when Judaculla jumped from the mountaintops on his farm and landed on the rock in the valley below. He had seven toes, and some viewers see a marking on the lower right side of the boulder as Judaculla's seven-toed footprint!

Some viewers see the markings in the picture below as a hand. But this marking, and every other one on Judaculla, can mean something different to each person who studies it.

Most archaeologists think that the markings on Judaculla are not a writing system that can eventually be read like Egyptian hieroglyphics or a phonetic alphabet, but that it may be possible to interpret the symbols.

Since no Cherokee has ever been able to explain what the markings on Judaculla mean, most researchers believe they were in place before the Cherokee established themselves in what is now Jackson County.

### Theories

Here are some of the theories that about Judaculla:

- **Map** — This is a very popular theory among the locals, and for good reason. They find unexplained marks on rocks in unexpected places, and many of the marks parallel present and past trails, roads and boundaries.

 The Smoky Mountain Times, a newspaper in Bryson City, North Carolina, reported on July 1, 1999, that Alan Brown of Bryson City found and photographed a "desk-sized" rock while hiking in the riverbed near the forks of the Little Tennessee and Tuckaseigee Rivers. Brown said the markings were a map of the area where he found it.
- **Memorial to a Peace Treaty** — Most researchers discount this theory, because there is nothing in the rich oral tradition of the Cherokees to support it.
- **Battle Plan** — But whose?
- **Religious Symbols**
- **Storytelling in Rock Art**
- **Tool to Teach the Inhabitants a Communication System**

**Visit Judaculla and Develop Your Own Theory!**

Judaculla Rock is off the beaten path, but worth the trip.

**Directions:** From US 74, take Exit 85 to Business Route 23 through Sylva.

Stay on 23, 1.3 miles to NC 107, then turn left on 107. Drive 8 miles south on 107 and look for this sign.

Photograph by Juanitta Baldwin

When you see this sign turn left — before you pass the sign — on Caney Fork Road, County Road 1737. Drive 2.5 miles, then turn left onto a gravel road, and drive 0.45 mile.

Judaculla Rock is on the right side of the road, and the parking lot is straight ahead. There are no rest rooms. There is a short trail down the slope to Judaculla, and a wooden viewing platform.

The small park that hosts Judaculla is home to a variety of tall trees, and wildflowers decorate the outer edges. Squirrels and birds are everywhere.

In this quiet and restful spot, you can send your imagination back in time to retrieve images of who wrote on Judaculla, and seek an interpretation of the message they left for us!

## Chapter 9
## Riddle of the Brown Mountain Lights

Many people who have seen the lights that frolic on Brown Mountain in North Carolina have tried to determine their origin, but as of 2002 the riddle remains unsolved.

Photograph courtesy Jaeme Haviland, Brown Mountain April 14, 2001

I can attest to the fact there are lights on Brown Mountain, because I have seen them. At the time I saw them, I had never heard of the mysterious, enigmatic nocturnal light phenomenon that has made this 2,750-foot peak of cranberry granite world-famous.

One balmy evening in September, my husband, Jesse, and I were traveling on the Blue Ridge Parkway in a motor home and stopped to walk our dogs. Twilight changed to darkness with surprising speed. Small, brilliant white and red lights that appeared in the distance, just below the crest of the mountains and just above the horizon, grabbed our attention.

At that time, we lived near several large civilian and military airports, and immediately assumed that planes or helicopters were in the area, and started to drive away. But we stopped when a cluster of yellow lights flickered among the trees, rose above them, and hovered for a few seconds before going out. We heard no sound, but attributed this to the distance from which we were viewing the lights.

Jesse has a private pilot's license. We have flown in all types of small planes and commercial aircraft all over the world, so after watching the lights for a while we concluded we were not seeing aircraft. But we had no clue as to the source of the impressive light show.

Neither of us experienced any hint of emotion beyond curiosity, and nothing alerted us that these lights are considered by many to be "unnatural," "paranormal," or "ghostly."

The next day we were chatting with a couple in the campground and told them about the beautiful unexplained lights we had seen the night before. They told us about the Brown Mountain lights, and said we had probably seen them, since several people had reported seeing them the same night.

We were intrigued, and have gone back along the Blue Ridge Parkway several times, armed with information and cameras, but we have not seen them again. I have amassed a large quantity of information about the lights and will share some of it in this chapter.

### Geologic Pedigree of Brown Mountain

Brown Mountain is in the Blue Ridge Mountains, which are part of the Appalachian chain. The unexplained lights that frolic on it are the only thing that distinguishes it from the mountains that surround it.

Most of Brown Mountain is in Pisgah National Forest, well off the beaten path. There are no scenic drives for regular cars or and buses, but there is an Off Road Vehicle Area, about 20 miles north of Morganton, North Carolina. Hiking is also a way to see Brown Mountain up close. But there are easily accessible vantage points from which to view the lights.

Wisemans View, 5 miles south of Linville Falls on State Road 1238, is a prime vantage point according to people who have seen the lights from more than one place. And in broad daylight the view is striking.

Wisemans View, Photograph courtesy National Forest Service

Lost Cove Cliffs overlook is a also good vantage point from which to view Brown Mountain. It is at Milepost 310 on the Blue Ridge Parkway.

The Brown Mountain lights have no regular performance schedule. They have been seen from dawn to dusk, and in all kinds of weather, even rain and snow.

One Pisgah National Forest employee said he had worked there for over 20 years and has yet to see the lights. When asked if he doubted their existence, he replied with a sly grin, "I don't dare. My wife and her mother have seen them."

### Bynum General Store

You can't see the lights on Brown Mountain from Bynum General Store, but the singing group the Brown Mountain Lights — Greg Bower, Janet Place, John Flowers, Pat McGraw and Jeff Hart — may be there. Check out their schedule on their Website, http://www.brownmountainlights.net.

The Brown Mountain Lights — Photograph courtesy Jeff Hart

## Scotty Wiseman Immortalized a
## Brown Mountain Lights Legend in Song

Wisemans View is named for McKamie Wiseman, a shrewd old mountaineer of Avery County. Scotty Wiseman, McKamie Wiseman's nephew, told one of the many legends about the Brown Mountain lights in his song "Legend of Brown Mountain Lights."

It was recorded by Tommy Faile in the 1960s, and topped the country music charts. The legend that Scotty Wiseman told is about the Brown Mountain landowner and his slave Jim.

### Legend of Brown Mountain Landowner and His Slave Jim

Brown Mountain was named after a Brown family, who owned a lot of land during the 19th century that included this mountain. The family owned slaves, and enjoyed the reputation of treating them well.

During the Civil War, one of the men in the Brown family fought in the Confederate army as a colonel. He was wounded in 1863 and came home. When he was well enough, he went for a day's hike and hunting on Brown Mountain, a place he knew well. He took a little food and water, and two lanterns.

Midnight came and the colonel had not returned. His faithful slave Jim took a lantern and went to Brown Mountain to look for him. Neither Jim nor the colonel ever returned. The family and their slaves searched the entire surface of Brown Mountain, but no trace of either of them has ever been found.

Shortly after the colonel and Jim disappeared, bobbing lights appeared on the mountain. The lights had never been seen before, and the family believed the lights were from the lanterns the colonel and Jim carried. They are trying to find their way home.

### Cherokee and Catawba Legend

The Cherokee and Catawba tribes were bitter enemies. In AD 1200, they fought a fierce battle in and around Brown Mountain. Both sides suffered a great loss of life.

Both tribes believe the lights are the spirits of maidens who loved young warriors, and of other distraught relatives, who are still searching for their loved ones.

### Amanda's Torch Still Flames

Amanda lived on high on Brown Mountain with her widowed father about 1775. She was lonely until a handsome young stranger from a village in the valley came into her life. His name was Caleb, and he too was lonely.

Caleb and Amanda fell in love. He asked her to marry him, and with her father's blessing she said yes. All was arranged, and on the evening Caleb was to come and take her away, she lighted a pine torch and went out to wait for him.

Caleb never came. Amanda and her father searched the trail and the whole mountain, but did not find him. Amanda's heart was broken, and her father could not comfort her.

Refusing to give up, every day at sunset Amanda lighted a pine torch and searched the mountain until her death. Her restless spirit still searches.

### Investigations of the Brown Mountain Lights

Scientific investigations into the cause of the Brown Mountain lights have been conducted since the early 20th century, and are still going on.

■ Gerald William de Brahm, was the U.S. government's surveyor general for southern North America during the 18th century made the first known official report of the Brown Mountain lights.

He observed them while surveying in North Carolina in 1771, and recorded a theory that some type of vapor or gas was ignited in random places and flamed brightly for a few seconds. This theory has been proven false.

- On October 11, 1913, the Geological Survey sent D.B. Sterrett to Brown Mountain to investigate and determine the origin of the lights. Sterrett apparently saw the lights immediately, because after only a few days he concluded that the lights were locomotive headlights from the railroad traffic on neighboring heights in the Brown Mountain area.

This explanation was too simple and prosaic to please anybody, especially those looking for some supernatural or unusual origin of the lights. The lights had been seen before there were railroads, and were seen after the great flood of 1916 while no trains were running in the vicinity.

- In 1922 the Geological Survey sent George R. Mansfield to conduct another investigation into the origin of the lights. His report was published in 1922 as Geological Survey Circular 646. It is 18 pages long, and refreshingly free of bureaucratic gobbledygook.

He concluded that the Brown Mountain Lights are not of unusual nature or origin. About 47 percent of the lights that the writer was able to study instrumentally were automobile headlights, 33 percent locomotive headlights, 10 percent stationary lights, and 10 percent brush fires. Mansfield's conclusion has not been accepted either by lay people or by the scientific world.

- Interest in investigating the Brown Mountain Lights lagged after 1922. In 1962 Three Morganton-area businessmen, Paul Rose, Howard Freeman, and R.M. Lineberger, wanted to capitalize on the tourists that Scotty Wiseman's ballad — "Legend of the Brown Mountain Lights" — was bringing to the area.

Rose, Freeman and Lineberger built a 50-foot tower near the top of Brown Mountain to photograph the lights. They were plagued by harsh weather. There are conflicting reports as to whether or not they made photographs. In any event, none of their photographs are known to exist.

One night the men were standing on the tower. Without warning, a sizzling ball of fire swooped around them. When it was gone, they were so dizzy and nauseated that they abandoned the project.

Assuming that the ball of fire was the same as the lights, this is only report I have found of a "close encounter" with the Brown Mountain Lights.

### Investigation by the Enigma Project

Michael A. Frizzell is research director for the Enigma Project, a Maryland-based phenomena-research association. He became interested in the Brown Mountain Lights after reading about them in Argosy magazine.

I corresponded with Mr. Frizzell about his investigations of the Brown Mountain Lights, and he said that he had been able to determine what they are not, but not what they are. Other projects now preclude him from making any investigations for some time to come.

In 1978 Frizzell joined forces with the Oak Ridge Isochronous Observation Network (ORION) of Oak Ridge, Tennessee, to "make some reason out of the Brown Mountain rhyme." ORION is not a government agency.

The first joint Enigma/ORION investigation took place during the first week of July 1978. Some twenty researchers went to Brown Mountain with a vast array of equipment. They saw the lights only one time — precisely at midnight — and they were on Chestnut Mountain, not Brown Mountain. Despite having state-of-the-art photographic equipment, they did not get any photographs, but did determine that the lights traveled at a speed of 37.5 miles per hour.

Four other joint investigations were conducted from 1980 to 1984, but they were not able to offer any explanation of the lights.

Lack of funding and technical problems have prevented any further Enigma/ORION investigations.

Frizzell wrote about these joint investigations, and other investigations, of the Brown Mountain Lights in a chapter in the book *True Tales of the Unknown — The Uninvited,* published by Bantam Books in 1989.

The ISBN is 0-553-28251-4, and it is hard to find.

**Oak Ridge Isochronous Observation Network Experiments**

ORION conducted an experiment/investigation of the Brown Mountain Lights in May 1977. The working theory was to determine whether reflected light could be the origin of the lights. A 500,000-candlepower arc light was placed in Lenoir, a city 22 miles east of Brown Mountain. When it was switched on, observers at 3.5 miles west of Brown Mountain saw an orb of light above the crest of the mountain.

ORION's conclusion was that some of the lights seen above the crest of Brown Mountain are refractions of artificial light. This did not explain the lights below the crest of the ridge, which are brighter and seen more often.

In July 1981 ORION detonated small charges on Brown Mountain to determine whether the lights seen below the crest of the mountain could be seismic in origin. The data they collected supplied conclusive evidence that they are not seismic in origin, because no artificially stimulated lights were recorded during any of the detonations.

## Investigation by League of Energy Materialization and Unexplained Phenomena Research (L.E.M.U.R.)

During two weeks in November 2000 the League of Energy Materialization and Unexplained Phenomena Research (L.E.M.U.R.), a team based in Asheville, North Carolina, investigated and photographed the Brown Mountain Lights on video and still shots.

This is the first time the lights have been recorded successfully on video.

This photograph was made by Brian Irish, vice president of L.E.M.U.R., and is printed here with their permission.

L.E.M.U.R. president Joshua P. Warren says the team is studying the video to determine places on the Brown Mountain Ridge to go for more intense study.

In 2002, the Travel Channel, in cooperation with L.E.M.U.R. filmed a segment on the Brown Mountain Lights to air on the show "Mysterious Journeys." It aired the first time in March 2002. For more information, visit:
http://www.brownmountainlights.com.

## Others Interested in the Brown Mountain Lights

The Brown Mountain Lights have been used by authors Nancy Roberts, John Parris, Andy Anderson, and John Harden to add mystery and suspense to their work.

The lights were a segment on "The X-Files" show on May 9, 1999 titled "Field Trip."

## Will the Riddle of the Brown Mountain Ever Be Solved?

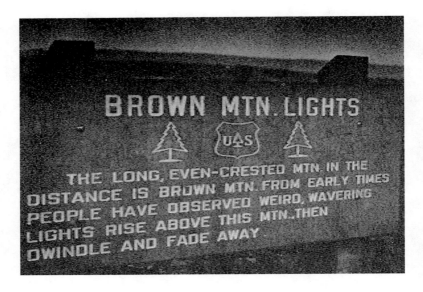

The message in this picture of a road sign on the Blue Ridge Parkway is accurate as this book goes to press in 2002.

Will the riddle of the Brown Mountain Lights ever be solved? Or will they forever remain in the collage of natural mysteries about the world, for those who come after us to enjoy?

# Chapter 10
# Whose Bones Were in Our Barn?

This barn was built about 1890 in Sevier County, Tennessee. My husband, Jesse, and I bought it about a century later. The old barn is gone now, a victim of urbanization.

Photograph by Jesse Baldwin

I had never owned a barn, and spent many happy hours exploring it with our beloved Basenjis, Lady and Duke. Jesse had lived on a huge farm in Tennessee, with lots of barns, until he was about ten years old and did not join in our forays.

And that turned out to be fortuitous, because what we discovered in our old barn is the stuff of headlines and best sellers. If Jesse had been with us, he'd have caused a bunch of trouble, because he's a compulsive stickler for getting to the bottom of everything.

One previous owner, Stanley Cate, lived nearby. He was in his eighties, and loved to talk about the old days. He told great stories about what happened while he and his wife, Ethel, owned the barn. They used it primarily for cattle and to process tobacco for market.

## What We Discovered

It was a bright and sunny day, and Duke, Lady and I were exploring the barn. For several weeks, they had dug in a spot near the wall. The soil was soft because the rain would blow in through a hole in the side of the barn. Between digs, the rain and wind removed most of the soil they dug, so gradually the hole got wider and deeper.

Stanley walked down the road while Duke and Lady were digging furiously. I walked out to the road, and after a brief inquiry about his health, asked him to come in and tell me if I could expect the dogs to unearth a hidden treasure.

He exclaimed with a wide grin, "I wondered how long it would take you to find it."

I had made a path by trampling the weeds. Stanley negotiated it gingerly with his walking stick and told me, "Tell Jesse to get these weeds cut and baled, because they made good hay. He can sell it."

Stanley stopped several times and used his walking stick as a pointer to remind me where the old pond he had dug to water his cattle, deep gullies, pasture and crops used to be.

As we entered the barn, I said, "Duke and Lady have dug up a couple of small bones, but no gold yet."

When Stanley saw where the dogs were digging, he looked startled, and I saw the beginning of tears in his eyes. Uneasy thoughts crowded into my brain, but I asked lightly, "Are the weeds aggravating your allergies?"

He shook his head. "No, not yet." He pondered for a few moments, then asked, "Did you say the dogs dug up some little bones?"

There was something in his voice, and the pained expression on his face, that alarmed me. "Yes," I answered, hoping he'd not notice. "Animal bones, don't you guess?"

Stanley looked at me searchingly for several moments, then said, "My guess is that they are human bones."

I thought he was joking, and I laughed, "Did you bury bodies here in the barn?"

He held up his hands and shook he head. "Oh, Lord, no! But if you let Duke and Lady keep on digging the way they're going at it, they may dig up a man's skeleton."

The expression on Stanley's face told me he was not joking. I tensed and waited.

He took a sharp anguished breath and inquired with caution, "What did you do with the bones?"

I replied as casually as I could, "I tossed them out in the field to keep Duke and Lady from eating them." A chill in my spine made me blurt out, "Stanley Cate, you're just making this up to tease me!"

Silence hung between us for a few seconds. Stanley's brows were knitted in pain. At last, in a strained voice, he said, "Believe me, *I am not!*" I know you write mysteries...I might put you on to one." He glanced quickly at the dogs, who were still digging furiously. "On conditions."

Curiosity surged, and I blurted out, "I agree."

Stanley, with a face like the aged Saint Peter and the obduracy of a cavalry sergeant, tapped my arm with his walking stick and shouted, "How can you agree when you don't know what the conditions are?"

I remember answering with a slow smile, "I assumed that the conditions would be the same as you always impose when you tell me things about folks in Sevier County that they would rather no one know — that I not tell who told me. And some things, I'm not to tell unless I outlive you."

"Not this time," he said sternly. "If I tell you why I think Duke and Lady dug up some human bones out of that hole, you must not tell Jesse or anyone until I am dead and gone. Usually I don't mind if you tell him. After I'm gone, you can tell God and everybody."

For a few seconds, thunderbolts of "agree" and "forget it" bounced around in my head. Stanley appeared to be an honorable man, but I'd been in this world long enough to know that appearances are not synonymous with reality. But these mental gymnastics were silly. There was space in my Secrets Pouch for anything he might tell me, so I said firmly, "Stanley, if I outlive you, I promise not to tell until you are dead and gone. As always, I have my tape recorder with me to make notes. May I record our conversation?"

There was a slight but definite pause. "Okay, if you promise never to let anyone hear it while I'm alive."

I raised my right hand and said in a serious tone, "I, Juanitta Baldwin, friend of Stanley Cate, do solemnly swear that I will not tell the tale I am about to hear, or play the tape of the tale Stanley is about to tell, unless I survive Stanley. In the event I go to my reward before he does, this tape will be among the things in my safety deposit box with instructions that the administrator of my estate destroy it without playing the tape or reading the transcript!"

Stanley laughed. Without further ado, we sat down on the steps to the barn loft and Stanley told me an incredible tale. Sadly, I am now free to tell "God and everybody," because he has gone to his reward.

☠☠☠☠

"It started on a bright, sunny Sunday morning in September," he said, then stopped as if lost momentarily in the past.

"I was here at the barn, feeding the cattle and feeling real happy. We'd had a good crop, me and Ethel, and the cattle were healthy. It was so quiet and the air was so clear. I was enjoying God's handiwork, and I had to remind myself to get a move on so Ethel and I could get to church on time.

"This was probably '47 or '48, the best I remember. About the time I was putting in the last of the feed, I heard a truck drive up and stop. I didn't recognize the motor, but I thought it was a neighbor because at that time the road was a dirt road that ran across my farm to link up with people across the hill.

"When I walked out of the barn, a man I did not recognize got out of a black Chevrolet pickup and walked toward me. He was a tall, rawboned white man, wearing a seersucker suit, straw hat, and sunglasses. When he got close, I saw he was about my age.

"I called out, 'Howdy,' and waited, wondering who he was and what he wanted.

"He said, 'Morning,' and extended his hand. 'I'm Red Wiggins. Do you own this barn?'

"I shook his hand and told him I was Stanley Cate, that I owned this barn, and asked why he wanted to know.

"Wiggins looked at the barn, then back at me before he answered. Then he said, 'I was in these parts about 1927, and spent a hell of a night in this barn. Did you own it then?'

"I told him, 'No, not that far back, but I think a relative of mine, who went by the name "One Arm Cate" because he lost his arm in some kind of accident, owned it in 1927. Why did you spent a night in this barn?'

"Wiggins shook his head and said, 'Mr. Cate, it's a long story. I'm not too proud of what happened. I've tried to forget it, but I can't. I've tried to get enough religion to blot it out, but that ain't worked either. I decided to come back, see if the barn was still here, and try to make peace with my Maker where it all happened. Will you let me go in the barn and look around?'

"By that time, Juanitta, I didn't know what to think or do. I felt uneasy about letting him go in my barn with me going off to church. So I told him my wife and I were going to church and invited him to go with us, then we'd come back and he could look around. Then, I remember telling him that maybe he could pray some and talk to the preacher about what was tormenting him. He said he'd like to go in the barn and pray. I thought he might just be plain crazy.

"I was used to hard work on the farm, and felt I was stronger than he was, so I wasn't afraid of him. Common sense told me he probably wasn't up to anything bad or he would have waited until nobody was around and sneaked into the barn.

"But by that time I wanted to know what kind of sin he'd committed in the barn, so I gave him a choice. Either he could go with us to church and we'd come back and go in the barn together, or he could come another time. In plain talk, I let him know I wanted to be around when he was in my barn.

"Wiggins said okay. I told him where the church was and he said he'd meet us there. I told Ethel on the way that a man named Red Wiggins had come by the barn, and that he'd been around here years ago and wanted to see how things had changed. I never breathed a word about his wanting to go into the barn because Ethel would have had a fit.

☠☠☠☠

"Wiggins was at the church, and I was relieved that he hadn't gone back to the barn. Singing had started, so I didn't have to introduce him to anybody but Ethel. Wiggins sat down in the back row, and Ethel and I went closer to the front where we always sat. In those days there was no such thing as a nursery, so I always ended up holding somebody's child to give the parents a break and keep them quiet.

"The preacher's sermon was on the need to repent of sin. When he gave the altar call, I half expected to see Wiggins come down the aisle, but he didn't.

"After the service ended, the preacher walked to the back of the church to shake hands with everybody. By the time I looked around, Wiggins was shaking the preacher's hand, and they were talking. Wiggins had gone on out in the churchyard by the time I shook the preacher's hand. He was standing by his truck smoking a cigarette. I went over and asked him if he still wanted to go to the barn, and he said he did. I told him I'd take Ethel to a neighbor's house where we'd been invited for Sunday dinner, and meet him up at the barn in about half an hour. He said okay and thanked me.

"I didn't exactly lie to Ethel, but I didn't tell her I was going to meet Wiggins at the barn. I told her I needed to check on Old Daisy, one of the cows who had been acting funny. She had been acting funny, but had seemed okay that morning. If I'd told Ethel about Wiggins, she'd have quizzed me, because she distrusted almost everybody, and she probably would have insisted on going too.

"After I dropped her off at the neighbor's house, I went by my house and picked up a pair of coveralls to keep my suit clean. I'd have changed, but I had to go to that Sunday dinner after I met with Wiggins. Ethel would have bawled me out if I'd showed up in work duds. I went to the barn, and Wiggins was waiting in his truck."

Stanley pointed his walking stick upward, and said with a devilish grin, "I never told Ethel about what happened with Wiggins here at the barn, so if she's up there listening, I'll hear about it when I get there."

Stanley's facial expressions and choice of words allowed me to vicariously relive his encounter with Red Wiggins. I was so spellbound that I had not noticed that Duke and Lady had stopped digging and were resting on the dirt they had piled up, but Stanley had, and he departed from his narrative to comment.

"I'd never seen or heard of a dog that can't bark until you moved here," he said, pointing his walking stick at Duke and Lady. "Basenjis are sure different from the farm dogs we always had, but I can see why they are good hunters. You and Jesse treat them like kids, but you ought to let them loose to hunt rabbits once in a while. We used to eat rabbits and squirrels. Have you ever tasted them?"

I wasn't the least bit interested in rabbits or squirrels at that moment, and sensed that Stanley was either stalling or enjoying center stage. Either way, I wanted him to get on with his story.

"Stanley," I said, trying to hide my impatience, "You know good and well I am a vegetarian! Let's talk about rabbits and squirrels another time. Right now, tell me what you and Red Wiggins did in this barn!"

He grinned, and resumed his narrative.

☠☠☠☠

"One thing struck me. Wiggins was clean-shaven. When he took off his hat at church, I noticed that he had a full head of snow-white hair. When we met back up at the barn I asked him a couple of questions before we went in. I asked if 'Red' was a nickname, and where he was from.

"He told me, 'Yeah, it's a nickname. My mama named me Peter, and always prayed I'd be like the Peter in the Bible. She got furious when my older brothers and sisters called me

"Pete" so they changed it to "Red" because I was as redheaded as a peckerwood. Mama didn't like that, but it stuck.

" 'I was born in Fontana, North Carolina, but I've lived most of my life in Canton. Fontana went under the water when the TVA build Fontana Dam. I've worked for Champion in the lumber yard for over twenty years. I was too young for the first World War, and too old and unhealthy with lung trouble for World War II. My wife died last year, and I went to live with a daughter in Asheville who lost her husband in the war.'

"I had a queer feeling about our going in the barn, but I'd told him he could. An old granny woman used to say she had 'bad feelings' when she was with certain people, and we'd always laughed at her. But I never did after that. I could not go back on my word, so I remember saying, 'Let's go in the barn and see if you can make the peace you want.'

"We came into the barn right over there," Stanley said, pointing his cane toward the front entrance. "Red took off his sunglasses and stopped to let his eyes adjust. Then he walked straight to where your dogs have been digging. I stopped about twenty feet behind him and didn't say a word, just watched. He was either a crazy man or he'd been in the barn before, because he didn't need directions.

"At that time there were seven big rocks over there. And I mean big," he said, making a circle with his arms. "I couldn't reach around any of them. They were there when I bought the place. I figured somebody wanted to get them out of the field and brought them in here to sit on or to brace the wall.

"Wiggins stood like he'd taken root and stared at the rocks for a few minutes, but didn't say a word. Then, quick as lightning, he set himself in motion and dropped to his knees in front of the center rock. He leaned forward, cradled his head in his arms, and began to sob."

We heard a tractor coming up the road, and I turned off

the tape recorder until it passed. Ordinarily we'd have gone out for a chat. "Stanley," I said with a note of urgency, "if anybody comes by, you may miss your 9 o'clock bedtime tonight, because I won't sleep a wink until I hear the end of this tale!"

He nodded, and as he resumed speaking I noted that the pupils of his eyes were wide, as if he was reliving the shock of that day long ago. "Juanitta, I was flabbergasted, and I can almost see him now. I had no more idea what he was doing than the man in the moon, but I got such an awful feeling that I could feel the hair on my neck stand up.

"Here was this stranger acting like he was kneeling at the manger of Christ. I walked a little closer to him but kept quiet.

"Red sobbed so hard his body shook, just like a woman. Men cry, but all of them I know try to hold themselves tight. Women bawl with their whole body."

Despite the gravity of what Stanley was describing, a grin must have escaped from my brain to my face, and he noticed. I didn't say a word, but made amends by nodding affirmatively so Stanley would not lose his momentum.

He said emphatically, "Well, they do! Anyway, after about five minutes, Red's sobs started tapering off. I went over and put my hand on his shoulder and said something like, 'Red, tell me what happened that left you with such a burden.'

"Red tried to get up, but he kind of fell to one side like he was feeling weak or sick. I got hold of his arm and helped him up. He seemed unsteady on his feet, and I put my right arm around his shoulder and guided him to these steps where we are sitting now.

"We sat down, and he wiped his eyes and face with the handkerchief he'd taken from his pocket when he'd been sobbing at the rocks. I noticed that it was embroidered with the initials PW, and this made me think that maybe he'd told me his real name — Peter Wiggins.

"I asked him to tell me what happened in the barn when he was here. Red Wiggins looked me straight in the eye and said, 'Me and two other guys killed a man and buried him under those big rocks over there.'"

Stanley clenched his teeth together. "Like I told you before, I did not think he was up to anything bad or he would have just sneaked in the barn. But I'd demanded that I be here when he was, and boy, oh boy, I got more than I bargained for!

"There I was face to face with a man who says he helped kill a man and buried him in my barn. I didn't know if I wanted him to tell me any more or just leave and let me go on to Sunday dinner, and forget I ever met Red Wiggins. But it was not my choice, Red had decided to take his burden to me and the Lord — in my barn — and leave it here!"

Stanley's eyes were more alert than I'd ever seen them. He'd had a heart attack, and possibly a stroke, shortly before I met him, and at times his speech was labored. But the adrenaline was pumping, and he was speaking with ease. Although I was bursting with questions, I vowed to keep quiet before his adrenaline ran dry.

"Now, where was I?" he asked.

I replayed his last words on the tape recorder to answer his rhetorical question.

☠☠☠☠

Several shades of expression passed over Stanley's face before he spoke with a definite grimace. "After Red said he'd killed a man, I guess I'd rocked back and stared at him, horrified-like, because he said, 'I won't try to hurt you.'

"It took me a few minutes to figure out what to say to him. From the look in his eyes, my gut told me he was telling me the truth. I finally said, 'You say it's been a long time. Maybe you're in the wrong barn.'

"Red looked me square in the eye and said, 'No, this is the barn. I had half hoped the rocks would be gone and I could tell myself I tried but couldn't find the right one. But the rocks are right there, and I've come back full of the best intentions to make my wrong as right as I can.'

" 'The three of us worked together as lumberjacks. We swore an oath to each other to take this secret to our graves. The other two guys are dead, and as far as I know they kept their oath. One was killed in less than a year after we murdered the man when a tree fell wrong and crushed him. The other fellow managed to get a job as a merchant seaman during World War II. The ship he was on was sunk on the way to Europe.'

" 'I've broken my sworn oath by telling you, but they are dead and gone and can't be hurt now by what I do. And I'll never tell their names. Mr. Cate, I never thought I was the kind of man who would need so desperately to discharge my guilt by an emotional confession. But when I came back face to face with those rocks, I found out I am. Mr. Cate, do you think I'll burn in Hell if I don't tell the law?'

Stanley paused for breath. He looked pale and rigid, but he braced his back against the wall and continued. "That question was a nightmare, and I thought about it for a while before I answered him. It had been so long, that I didn't see any good that could come from going to the law. We only had a sheriff. He was lazy and everybody knew he was on the take. Nine out of ten he wouldn't do anything. But if he saw a chance to make hay out of this before the election that was coming up in November, he'd round up some farmers and they'd wreck my barn.

"Red stared at me while I was thinking, and began to weep again...still like a woman with his handkerchief."

Stanley cut his eyes at me, as if deliberately for a reprieve, but I made a brusque gesture to say, — Get on with it!

His expression lightened faintly, but he spoke stiffly. "I told Wiggins that I believed he had the best intentions to make his wrong completely right, and the one to make it right with to stay out of Hell was God, not the law.

"It took him a few moments to overcome his surprise, but I could see that my answer pleased him. He said heartily, 'I've got to be honest and tell you that is what I have prayed you would say. I'm not hankering to open up a hornet's nest for you or myself, but I'm not hankering to go split Hell wide open one of these days. I've asked forgiveness for years, and again a few minutes ago. If that's enough, I will take my leave and trouble you no more, Mr. Cate.' He started to stand up.

"The common-sense thing for me to have done was jump up, shake his hand and hope never to see him again, but I am too curious for my own good. I said quickly, 'Red, I'm glad you got right with God about this, but if you're telling me the truth — and I believe you are — chances are that I have a body in my barn. I can tell you, as God is my witness, that I intend to let that body stay under those rocks. I won't be running to the law and take a chance of them wrecking my barn, or accusing me of burying it. So, be fair with me, before you go, tell me who was killed and why.'

### Murder in the Barn

"Red turned pale at my direct question, but he answered, 'Well, sir, I don't know who we killed. As I told you, we worked in a lumber camp, and we stayed in cabins just over the North Carolina line. It was Saturday night. We were three young bucks out for a good time over in Cocke County. We went to a house where they had plenty of moonshine, pickin' and singin', dancin', and lots of wild gals.

" 'We caroused until about midnight, and by the time we started home all three of us were as high as Georgia pines. It was pouring down rain. A guy we'd talked to inside had asked for a ride to go to our camp and ask for a job. The guy who owned the car said okay. Being drunk, the driver got lost and we ended up here at your barn. The big door was open, and the barn seemed empty. We were about out of gas. The guy always kept a 10-gallon drum of gas, so he said he'd drive in and we could fill up in the barn so we could stay dry.

" 'We lit a couple of lanterns. After we filled the tank, we got into an argument, and that turned into a drunken brawl.

" 'The argument started when the guy who had asked for a ride called the driver a name he hated. He was as strong as a bull and as mean as the devil. He swore at the guy, grabbed a pitchfork and threatened him. Me and the other guy were just drunk enough to egg them on. They circled each other for a while, and then the driver stuck the pitchfork in the guy's chest. He didn't bleed much, and he didn't live long.'

### The Murdered Man Was Buried in the Barn

" 'After sobering up enough to realize what we'd done, we decided to bury him under those rocks, and never tell anybody. And we did.'

" 'We never looked in his pockets to see if he had any identification. It was self-preservation. If we learned his name, somewhere down the line it might touch a chord of memory and give us away. One thing that has come to bear down on me is the grief we caused his family, if he had one.'

" 'That's the whole story, Mr. Cate. I've made peace with God the best I can. I don't see that digging up that body will help anybody now, and you seem to agree with me. That said, I thank you for your kindness. I'll be on my way, and you can get on to your Sunday dinner.'

"We stood and shook hands, but didn't talk any more. We'd said it all. He got in his truck and left. I felt agitated, but the deed was done. I watched him drive out of sight before I left. I never tried to find Red Wiggins, and I never heard from him again. For that, I can tell you, I thanked God every Sunday morning for a long, long time!"

I said, "You must have been in the barn for longer than it would have taken you to check on Old Daisy. I'm surprised Ethel didn't come looking for you, or send somebody."

Stanley replied, "You're a city girl. On a farm, things don't move so fast. And besides, Ethel was busy catching up on the gossip. But just to keep me in line, after she found out that Old Daisy was okay, she gave me a tongue-lashing for being so late for Sunday dinner."

### After Peter Wiggins' Pilgrimage

I blurted out, "Did you move the rocks to see if he'd really done that? What happened to them?"

Stanley laughed as if my questions were absurd, and said earnestly, "No, I didn't move the rocks. After that Sunday, I wanted them to stay right where they were, and I didn't go near them except when I had to. They were there when I sold the barn, and it was years before I saw they were gone.

"I asked Hal Hodges, the fellow you bought the barn from, about them, and he said he thought the developer I sold the farm to got the county to move them out and crush them when they took over the road.

"Hal, you will remember, was a paraplegic, and never saw the barn after he bought it. And before you ask me, he didn't say anything about them finding bones when they moved the rocks, and I didn't ask!"

I said emphatically, "Stanley, you must have told somebody about this."

"Oh, I did, right after it happened," he answered soberly. "I told my preacher and my lawyer, because they're not supposed to blab, but I swore them to lifetime secrecy anyway. They used fancy words, but I got the message to keep my trap shut! And I have, until you and your dogs came along. Remember, if you go blabbing this, the law may want to come digging in your barn!"

I said, "You made me promise not to blab! If you want to change your mind, maybe we can write the story and you'll get to be famous. Jesse thinks we'll have to have the barn torn down, so he won't be concerned about them digging."

He told me with a hearty laugh, "Keep the offer open."

After Stanley told me about the possibility that Duke and Lady might dig up human bones, I never again let them dig where he said the rocks used to be.

### Ashes to Ashes and Dust to Dust

The urbanization of our area accelerated. Jesse became concerned that our barn was an attractive nuisance, and it should be taken down. Although it gave me heartburn — big time — I had to agree.

Phil Johnson, assistant chief of the Northview Volunteer Fire Department, contracted to take the barn down. He took a lot of it down, but it was so difficult that he decided to do a controlled burn.

Stanley had been very ill, but he had recovered enough to be there. He and I watched the fire and speculated what it might do to the skeleton if Red Wiggins had told the truth about helping to bury a body in the barn.

Neither of us could think of a logical motive for him to tell such a tale, and kneel and sob at the rocks. We agreed it was so incredible it was probably true. We watched it end in silence — ashes to ashes and dust to dust.

Photograph by Juanitta Baldwin

I took this picture during the controlled burn of the barn. Left to right, Blackie in Eric's Johnson's arms, Phil Johnson, Stanley Cate with his cane, and Jesse Baldwin.

### I Miss You, Stanley

Stanley Cate was one of the first people Jesse and I met when we moved to Kodak. His warm welcome to us as "outsiders" helped ease our transition into our new home.

We visited him often, and as we drive by his old home we still feel a twinge of pain that we can't stop in for a chat.

I miss you, Stanley, and your incredible stories! You epitomized these paraphrased lines from Sam Walter Foss' poem.

- *You lived in a house by the side of the road,*
  *And you were a friend to man!*
  *...and to me!*

## Chapter 11
## Melungeons — People of Mystery

> The Melungeons are people of mystery. No one has solved the puzzle of how English speaking people, who practiced Christianity, got to the Smoky Mountains before the earliest explorers in the recorded history of the United States.

The unsolved mystery of the Melungeons has a particular personal facet for me. I heard the word Melungeon for the first time about ten years ago, during a conversation with my mother's sister, my Aunt Sarah.

She was telling stories about her parents, my maternal grandparents. Both of them had died before I was born, and I know very little about them. Perhaps this is because I've never been really interested in my family history.

Aunt Sarah was mischievous by nature, so she told stories that others whispered only to confidants. On this occasion she was telling me about a visit with an aged great-aunt, Laura Simons. They had not seen each other in almost thirty years, so a cousin was helping to establish that Aunt Sarah was one of John Shepherd's daughters.

Aunt Laura peered at Sarah and asked, "Are you one of his legitimate daughters, or one of the illegitimate ones?"

Aunt Sarah said she was taken aback, and stammered, "I guess I'm one of the legitimate ones! I don't know anything about my daddy having illegitimate children."

"Well," Aunt Laura replied, "that's about what I'd expect you to say. If you don't know about all your illegitimate half-brothers and sisters, it's high time you did."

Aunt Sarah said she was insulted and retorted, "Then why don't you tell me about them?"

She said Aunt Laura seemed to take great pleasure in reciting the sins of her father. "You know your daddy had sawmills all over several counties in western North Carolina and eastern Tennessee. He always was a lady's man, and you may as well know he even got a Melungeon pregnant, and the talk was that she had twins, a boy and a girl. What a stink that caused! And there were others."

I interrupted. "What is a Melungeon?"

Aunt Sarah replied, "A group of people who live in the Tennessee mountains. They are not Indians, but may be part Indian, because they have darker skin than regular white people. Nobody knows where they came from, or if God just created them like Adam and Eve and put them there. You love mysteries, so you can check this one out at the library. I don't know much about them."

"Do you know if what Aunt Laura said about your daddy fathering twins with a Melungeon woman is true?"

Aunt Sarah grinned, "I don't know. I thought about asking some kinfolks who knew Judge Lewis Shepherd, one of Daddy's cousins down in Chattanooga, but never did. Lewis won a big court case for a Melungeon girl. I don't remember the details, but it was about her inheriting some money, and he got it for her. I decided to let that sleeping dog lie."

I had no interest in my grandfather's possible adultery, or illegitimate progeny, but I was hooked on the unsolved mystery of the Melungeons. Many people are seeking to solve this mystery, and I follow it regularly in a variety of sources, particularly the World Wide Web.

This chapter is not intended to be either comprehensive or authoritative, but just to share enough information to stimulate interest in other unsolved-mystery addicts.

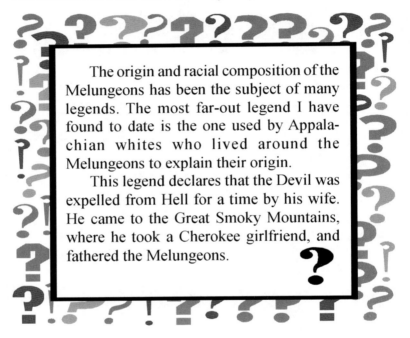

> The origin and racial composition of the Melungeons has been the subject of many legends. The most far-out legend I have found to date is the one used by Appalachian whites who lived around the Melungeons to explain their origin.
>
> This legend declares that the Devil was expelled from Hell for a time by his wife. He came to the Great Smoky Mountains, where he took a Cherokee girlfriend, and fathered the Melungeons.

**Explorers Discovered the Melungeons in the 17th Century**

When explorers pushed into the Appalachians, beginning in the 17th century, they discovered a group of people whose origins remain an unsolved mystery.

Most of them lived in eastern Tennessee, but there were a few in Kentucky and Virginia. They had established an orderly agrarian society in the fertile valleys, and sheltered themselves in cabins.

The people had English surnames, spoke an Elizabethan English dialect with a mountain cadence, practiced the Christian religion, and called themselves "Portyghee." This word sounded like a corruption of "Portuguese," but the explorers at the time did not appear to give any credence to the possibility that these people had their roots in Portugal.

### Physical Characteristics of the Melungeons

Most of the people had black hair and dark eyes, but a few had blonde or red hair and very striking blue or blue-green eyes. The explorers described the people as having skin that was "not white," "not black," "not Indian red," but a mixture of these colors. This description probably resulted in the people being called "Melungeons," from the French *melange*, a mixture.

There are many other possible explanations for the name "Melungeon," some serious, some amusing.

Dr. N. Brent Kennedy, vice chancellor for development and college relations at the University of Virginia's College at Wise, a prominent researcher of the Melungeons, says the name Melungeon is derived from the Arabic "Melun-Jinn," meaning one who has been abandoned by God and is a cursed soul.

That seems so sad that I was happy to find another theory which smacks of good humor. Michael Edward Nassau (who changed his name from McGlothlen in 1997), author of *Melungeons and Other Mestee Groups*, says his favorite word for an origin of the name Melungeon is *melongene*, a French word for eggplant!

In correspondence with Edward Nassau, Dr. Kennedy used the salutation, "Dear Eggplant!"

Mr. Nassau has published his work on the World Wide Web, and it can be read and/or downloaded free.

## Theories About the Origin of the Melungeons

Every theory I found has its supporters and its detractors. There is a great deal of research being done by highly competent people, but no theory has been proved. Hybridization of people and their languages has occurred since the first human drew a breath, and this wreaks havoc with theories.

Here are some of the most popular traditional theories of the origin of the Melungeons:

- Survivors from the Lost Colony of Roanoke Island in North Carolina, who intermarried with Native Americans.
- Tri-Racial Isolates: isolated group of intermarried white, black, and Native American populations.
- Descendants of the Welsh explorer "Madoc" who supposedly roamed in southern Appalachia in the 12th century.
- Survivors from Portuguese shipwrecks who mated with Native Americans.
- Descendants of one of the "lost tribes" of Israel.
- Descendants of early Carthaginian or Phoenician seamen who mated with Native Americans.
- Descendants of Mediterranean/Middle Eastern/East Indian people.

Discussion of all of these theories is beyond the scope of this book, but anyone interested in exploring one of these theories will find a wealth of information on the World Wide Web and in print. We'll take a look at two of them.

### The Carthaginian Theory

I began my research into the Melungeon mystery by checking the story Aunt Sarah had told about my grandfather's cousin, Lewis Shepherd, winning a court case in Chattanooga,

Tennessee, involving a Melungeon girl who was being denied an inheritance.

Her story was easily verified in official court records and legal references. Many of them titled the case the "Celebrated Melungeon Case." Lewis Shepherd was a prominent attorney and judge in Chattanooga at the time of his death in 1917 at the age of 61. This is a synopsis of the "Celebrated Melungeon Case."

In 1872 a Melungeon mother and a white father asked Lewis Shepherd, who was a struggling lawyer at the time, to help their daughter claim an inheritance. The daughter's inheritance was being challenged in court by cousins on the grounds that:

- Under Tennessee law only legitimate children can claim an inheritance.
- This cousin's, the defendant's, mother was Melungeon.
- Melungeons are part black.
- Black-white marriage was illegal under Tennessee law.
- Hence the defendant is illegitimate, and cannot inherit.

The theory of the cousins' case was considered to be based on law as solid as a rock. At that time, Tennessee law prohibited the marriage of a person one-sixth or more "Negro" to a white person.

Recognizing that it was futile to do battle on the merits of the Tennessee law on marriage between whites and blacks, Lewis Shepherd went into court with a case theory that was unexpected, and it produced unexpected results.

He espoused a new theory about the racial origin of the Melungeons. They were, in his judgment after investigations, descended from the Phoenicians of Ancient Carthage. Their ancestors had migrated from Portugal and had settled in South

Carolina about the time of the Revolutionary war. They moved into Tennessee, but had never intermarried with blacks. Hence, Lewis Shepherd argued:

- The defendant mother's was a descendant of a Carthaginian, without "Negro" blood.
- Therefore the mother's marriage to a white man was legal under Tennessee law.
- That law had to recognize the daughter born of that marriage as a legitimate child.
- As a legitimate child, the court must issue an order that she was a legal heir.

The court agreed with his arguments, and the girl's cousins, the plaintiffs, lost.

**Mediterranean/Middle Eastern/East Indian Theory**

For decades Melongeons have claimed to possess a partial Mediterranean/Middle Eastern/East Indian heritage.

This is the theory espoused by Dr. N. Brent Kennedy. He believes there is evidence that the Melungeons were settlers of either Ottoman Turks or Spanish/Turkish sailors who were stranded on American soil. Being trained survivalists, they pushed inland and intermarried with Cherokee, Creek, Powhatan, Catawba and Chickahominy women.

Dr. Kennedy has assembled a team of forty-two scientists and researchers who are studying all aspects of the Melungeon mystery. They are examining linguistics, medical genetics, diseases, dress styles, and physical traits to establish evidence of Melungeon ancestry.

They have found similarities in the languages that appear to be beyond chance. More than one thousand words in the Melungeon vocabulary have been traced to Arabic or Turkish origin. One example is "Alleghany," which in Turkish means "God's Spaciousness."

Dr. Kevin Jones, a molecular biologist and professor at the University of Virginia at Wise, is coordinating a comprehensive genetics study on the origins of the Melungeons with several other genetics labs and local area physicians.

The study is anticipated to be concluded before the end of 2002. Although Dr. Jones and the others will likely publish their findings in a refereed journal, a synopsis of the study results will be made available at an appropriate time on the Melungeon Heritage Association (MHA) Website: http://www.geocities.com/BourbonStreet/Inn/1024.

While this study probably will not give a definitive answer on the origin of the Melungeons, it is certain to shed new light on their ancestry and lead to further research.

Dr. N. Brent Kennedy is the author of the book *The Melungeons: The Resurrection of a Proud People.*

### Discrimination Against the Melungeons

The case of the Melungeon girl's having to go to court to claim an inheritance came about because whites reportedly discriminated against the Melungeons.

The majority of historians report that the white explorers seized the land from the Melungeons and drove most of them from the valleys to the ridge tops and poor or isolated land. But a few historians disagree, citing records that show that some of the Melungeon leaders owned a lot of good land. They cite records that seem to show that Melungeons, and other races of people who arrived in Tennessee in the 19th century, had to settle for less desirable land because the best land had already been claimed.

But there is no valid disagreement that the white majority passed laws to discriminate against the Melungeons. While the laws varied from state to state, they established a legal classification for Melungeons as free persons of color, but were denied rights to education, voting and judicial process.

The discrimination became so intense in central Appalachia that many Melungeons hid their backgrounds in a variety of ways. They adopted new surnames, became "Black Dutch," "Black Irish," or "Indian," or moved to a new community where they told everyone all their family were dead.

Legal discrimination lasted until antidiscrimination laws were passed by Congress in the 1960s. Social discrimination has not been legislated out of existence, so the process of eradication of that form of discrimination is still going on.

### Walk Toward the Sunset

An outdoor drama about the Melungeons, *Walk Toward the Sunset*, ran from 1969 to 1974 in Hancock County, Tennessee. It was written by Kermit Hunter (1910-2001), who wrote more than forty outdoor dramas and is perhaps the most widely performed playwright in the United States. Among his dramas are *The Lost Colony* and *Unto These Hills*.

This drama is credited by many as greatly improving people's understanding of the Melungeons. It also had a positive impact on some Melungeons. For the first time, many began to acknowledge their maligned heritage with pride.

The impact of the play was not accidental, but the direct result of Kermit Hunter's understanding of the Melungeon story and his great skill to tap into the minds and hearts of his audiences.

He is quoted as having said, "The story of the Melungeons is typical of some of the darker impulses in the American dream: those moments when the American dream gets crowded by white supremacy, the arrogance of wealth and position and power."

He illuminated each of these points as he told a story about certain whites driving some of the Melungeons from their valley farms to subsistence farming and moonshining.

The drama was created to alleviate poverty in Hancock County, one of the poorest counties in the United States. The movers and shakers realized they had two things going for them: some of the most beautiful mountains in the world, and the mysterious Melungeons. They used both, and the result was an economic and social success.

Although some consider the outdoor play strictly an economic venture, others believe it caused people to question racial stereotyping and bigotry.

### Mahala Mullins

Mahala Collins Mullins, nicknamed "Big Haley," is a famous Melungeon. She was born on March 30, 1824, in Hancock County, and died there in 1898.

Big Haley became famous for producing top-quality apple brandy and corn liquor, and selling it openly from her front door. And she was famous for her immense proportions. When she died, an obituary in a Columbia, Tennessee, newspaper read, "Mahala Mullins, famous fat woman of Hancock County, Tennessee, has died."

Reports of her weight range from 300 to 600 pounds. There is speculation that she suffered from elephantiasis. Whatever the reason, her weight gave her immunity from arrest! All the sheriffs knew where she was and that she was moonshining. Any one of them who came along could get a warrant for her arrest and serve it on her, but the action stopped there. Not one could solve the problem of getting her to the jail!

When Big Haley died, the story goes that either the chimney or a wall had to be removed to make room to carry her out in her bed, which had been boxed up like a coffin. She was laid to rest in a small cemetery near the house with some of her children who had died as infants.

### Mattie Ruth Johnson

I bought several books on the Melungeons — and read dozens more — while researching this story. One book that put a warm human face on the Melungeons mystery for me is Mattie Ruth Johnson's book *My Melungeon Heritage A Story of Life on Newman's Ridge*.

In 2002 Mattie Ruth Johnson works full time as a nurse, and is also an artist as well as a writer. The designer of the cover on her book used her painting the "Calf Lot Tree."

Her honest, wistful account of her life, blended so skillfully with her research findings on the Melungeons, prompted me to contact her for permission to include information about her book in this book, which she gave most graciously.

This is a quote from the Preface to her book, "The mysteries I leave to others. For example, an upcoming documentary on the Melungeons by Bill VanDerKloot and N. Brent Kennedy should give greater insight into some of the more recent findings regarding the origins of the Melungeons as a people. We shall see. Melungeons may have connections to many nationalities, including the Lost Tribe of Israel."

Mattie Ruth Johnson was born and raised in Hancock County, and is a descendant of several of the first known settlers in that county. Mahala Mullins is Mattie's great-great-great aunt on her mother's side of her family, and also her great-great-great aunt on her father's side of the family.

**Will the Melungeons Remain — A Mystery People?**

With so many people working to solve the mystery of the Melungeons, more information is bound to surface, but the true origins may remain an intriguing unsolved mystery.

I must agree with Mattie Ruth Johnson, whom I consider an expert on this mystery, in her conclusion: "Some mysteries may never be solved, but does it really matter?"

## Chapter 12
## Fairy Cross/Cross Stone —
## Facts, Folklore and Legends About It

This is a polished fairy cross. I have enlarged it so you can see its shape and texture. It was created by Nature's own hand in a quiet, sunny glade in the rugged foothills of the Blue Ridge Mountains in Virginia.

"Fairy cross" is a colloquial name for the mineral staurolite, from the Greek *stauros,* "cross," and *lithos,* "stone," in allusion to the common cross-shaped twins of the crystals with twinning crystals that form a cross.

Other colloquial names are "fairy stones," "fairy tears," "iron cross," and "cogwheel." But by whatever name, they are the stuff of myth and legends.

### The Geographical Myth

An enduring myth, in oral tradition and in print, is that fairy crosses are found only in southern Appalachia.

Of course, I believed this, since I'd learned this "fact" in school. It came as a shock to see beautiful fairy crosses on display in several museums in Russia! When I returned home, I set about resolving the discrepancy.

The resolution was that staurolite is found in Virginia, Tennessee, Georgia, Florida, North Carolina, New Hampshire, and Montana in the United States. It is also found in Italy Switzerland, Germany, Russia, Brazil, France and Scotland. And I'm confident this list is incomplete!

Every staurolite cross is different, but all of them, regardless of where they are found, are recognizable as some type of cross. Twins are cross (+) or X-shaped, and both can be present in one specimen. The most prevalent are shaped like the Roman or St. Andrew's crosses.

Those in the shape of the Maltese cross are rare, and consequently more highly prized. The design of the Maltese cross evolved from writing the first two Greek letters of Christ's name, Chi (x) and Rho (p), in a circle to create a cross.

### The Cross Is an Ancient Symbol

Although the cross is best known as a symbol of the Christian faith, its symbolism predates Christianity. Crosses dating back to 10,000 B.C. have been found on rocks and on the walls in a cave in the French Pyrenees.

Crosses have been symbols to represent different ideas to different cultures, but generally they are expressions of beliefs about the world, and spirituality.

### Fairy Cross Legends

There are many fairy cross legends in southern Appalachia that connect the tangible crosses with unseen spirits. And regardless of the shape of the fairy cross, the belief is that they are endowed with magical powers.

People who wear, or carry, a fairy cross are protected against witchcraft, disease and accident. It helps guard against negativity, draws wealth and energizes sexual drive.

Let's take a look at some of the fairy cross legends. To me, the greatest mystery about the legends is trying to fathom how they originated and survived.

## The Rain God Legend

The Rain God wanted to make his mighty presence known to the fairies who lived in southern Appalachia.

He caused it to rain, and the raindrops were in the form of crosses. The fairies were delighted and ran around picking them up. When everyone had a cross, they heard a mighty voice from the sky.

"I am your Rain God. Hold a cross I have sent, and listen to my important message." Everyone obeyed the command. They stood very still and listened.

The Rain God said, "I am the God of Rain. I send rain so you may have life. The crosses are my covenant to always send rain so you may have life. Wear a cross on a string around your neck at all times. It will give you great power, and be a remembrance of my great love for you."

## The Nunnehi Legend

The Nunnehi, according to Cherokee legend, are the immortals of the mountains. Some people call them "spirit people," and others call them "fairies."

The Great Spirit created them to live in harmony with Mother Earth. They are endowed with powers beyond those of human beings.

One of the most remarkable of these powers was the ability to make themselves visible or invisible at will. This power was possible because of a fairy cross they wore on a string around their necks. The Nunnehi had received the crosses when the Rain God had caused millions of tiny crosses to rain down on the Earth.

If a Nunnehi lost the cross, the power to be visible or invisible was lost. The lucky person finding the cross may not know what power they hold in their hand, and may never even try to become invisible!

### The Great Spirit Legend

One day a messenger from the Great Spirit came to where the fairies were making music and dancing under a full moon. Normally the messenger would have been invited to join the festivities, but the fairies sensed trouble.

"I have sad news," the messenger said. "You live in harmony with everything the Great Spirit has created, and have tried to teach the humans around you to do the same. Some humans do, but most are careless and evil. They mistreat the water, the mountains, and other living things.

"Because the humans are destroying the Earth, the Great Spirit is going to remove the evil humans from it. Fire, wind, and water will cleanse the Earth.

"A few humans, who have not been destructive of the Earth, will be allowed to live. The Great Spirit hopes they will be able to teach others respect for the Earth.

"You will not be harmed. When the cleansing is over, the Great Spirit says you may decide if you will live among the humans or forsake them forever."

The fairies were brokenhearted by this news and began to cry. As their tears touched the ground the Great Spirit turned them into crosses.

After the Earth was cleansed, the fairies decided not to live among the humans. But they told the humans, through visions and dreams, how the Great Spirit had turned their tears into crosses, and the crosses had magical powers to protect them from harm. They urged them to cherish the crosses and take care of the Earth.

The fairies were never seen again, but occasionally the humans could hear their music, and the soft tones of gentle conversation.

The humans have cherished the fairy tear crosses, and have passed them, and the story of their creation, along from generation to generation.

### Cherokee Tears Legend

In February 1838 the government of the United States began using force to drive the people of the Cherokee Nation from their homes in southern Appalachia to the Indian Territory now known as Oklahoma.

By October, great numbers were moving along the route that would be known as the "Trail of Tears." So great was the grief over the loss of their homeland that their tears turned to crosses.

This legend is a great tribute to the depth of suffering of the Cherokee by people in power. It took a long, long time, but this deed has been recognized by the American government for the crime that it was, and attempts to atone have been undertaken.

A Trail of Tears National Historic trail has been established. The trail covers more than 2,200 miles of land and water routes in nine states. There are many interpretive sites along the Trail to tell of what happened on "Nunahi-duna-dlo-hilu-i," the Trail Where They Cried, and many of the trail sites have a Website.

While it is doubtful that the tears the Cherokees shed became tangible crosses when they fell to the ground, no one can dispute the fact that they bore a cross in their hearts as long as they lived.

### Tears for Christ Legend

The fairies had gathered beside a great enchanted river to make music and dance. There was great joy and peace in their hearts until an elfin messenger arrived from far away.

She told them that Jesus Christ had been crucified. The fairies, and other creatures of the land, were so sad that they wept for a long time. As their tears fell upon the Earth, they crystallized into crosses.

### Fairy Stone State Park

Fairy stones were found in much greater abundance in western Virginia than anywhere else in the world. In 1936, Virginia opened Fairy Stone State Park near Stuart.

The legend that the crosses are the tears the fairies shed when they heard Christ had been crucified is in the promotional literature. Visitors may look for fairy stones and keep what they find. Information about the park may be obtained from their Website:
http://www.state.va.us/~dcr/parks/fairyst.htm.

### Who Believes That Fairy Crosses Protect?

Here is a list of prominent Americans who believed in the power of fairy crosses to protect them:
President Woodrow Wilson
Thomas A. Edison
Colonel Charles A. Lindbergh
President Theodore Roosevelt
Theodore Roosevelt not only carried a fairy cross, but named his ranch in North Dakota the Maltese Cross Ranch, and used it as a mark on his business documents.

Were all these people misguided by superstition about an inanimate object? Would their lives have been the same if they had not embraced its power? You decide!

### Staurolite/Cross Stone Collecting

Staurolites/cross stones have their own following in the world of professional and hobby mineral collecting. Others collect staurolite along with other minerals that form classic twins, such as fluorite, sanidine, microcline, harmotome, gypsum, cinnabar, spinel, and rutile.

To begin a collection, you can buy stones from a local or mail-order mineral dealer, or you dig your own. Many stories give the impression that the stones are just lying on the ground waiting to be picked up. It may have been true at one time, but that is rarely the case today.

There are commercial sites that charge a fee, usually very reasonable, for a dig. Fairy Stone State Park in Stuart, Virginia, is famous for its natural staurolite crosses that you can keep the crosses you are lucky enough to find.

There are wonderful resources on the World Wide Web about staurolite/cross stone/fairy cross collecting.

If you do not have access to the Web, check with your local library. A good place to begin is with publications by the Mineralogical Society of America.

### Lucky Fairy Cross Jewelry

If you opt for the protection of a fairy cross, you can wear it as jewelry. George Osborne crafts fairy crosses into necklaces and earrings, and sells them on the World Wide Web.

I found his site, The Lucky Fairy Cross, while researching for this book, and purchased a necklace. The cross I

**133**

Photograph courtesy George Osborne

received is about an inch long and pictured on the first page of this chapter.

George Osborne says the crosses are not always readily available, and suggests you contact him for availability at these addresses:
- Website: http://www.webspawner.com/users/fairycross
- E-mail: gosborn5785@earthlink.net, or georgeo_2002@yahoo.com
- PO Box 143, Grant, Florida 32949.

**Fairy Cross Quilt**

Madeline Smith's high school Latin teacher gave her a fairy cross necklace as a graduation present. The teacher was from North Carolina, and he had acquired the stone there, then had a craftsman cap the ends and attach a link for a chain.

Many years later, she was at a craft show and saw a full-sized-quilt being used as a tablecloth. She was fascinated by the pattern, because it looked like her fairy cross necklace. She asked the lady who had the quilt what the pattern was, but she did not know because a friend had brought it to her from Nova Scotia.

Mrs. Smith, being an expert quilter, sketched the pattern, went home and made her own Fairy Cross Quilt pattern, and the wall-hanging-size quilt pictured here.

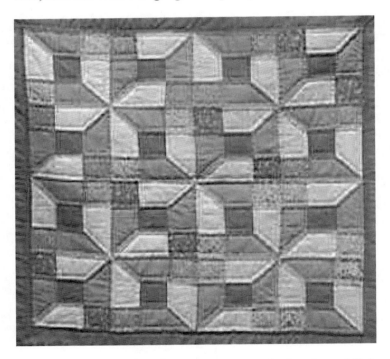

She most graciously gave me permission to publish pictures of her quilt and the quilt pattern.

Unfortunately, the size constraints of this book do not permit me to include the pattern, which is several pages in length.

## Chapter 13
## Sarbe Springs Haints

Sarbe Springs is on Alarka Road, about three miles from Exit 64 off State Highway 74, in Swain County, North Carolina. This is how it looked in the bright June sunlight.

Photograph by Juanitta Baldwin

I went there hoping to meet one or more of the Sarbe Spring Haints that I've heard about all my life from my mother, other members of her family, and many residents of the Alarka community. My mother grew up in a home on Alarka Creek, about two miles from Sarbe Springs.

When I parked on the side of the road and began making pictures, the melody of Alarka Creek could be heard in the distance. Butterflies were feasting on the wildflowers. The moss on the rocks around the springs was thin, and the springs were almost dry. I later learned that a resident had installed a pump and used the spring water in his home. Except for a better road and new utility poles, Sarbe Springs looked about the same as when I was a child shivering with excitement at the prospect of seeing a haint.

I went to Sarbe Springs because I had found a personal account of an encounter with a haint there. It was written in 1927 by Oliver Shepherd, a distant relative. When an elderly pack-rat aunt died in 1982, she left boxes and boxes of papers. My mother stored them in her basement but never went through them. I am working my way through them, and found this great story. It is printed below just as Oliver wrote it, but I couldn't resist adding a few pictures.

Oliver Shepherd
Alarka, North Carolina
October 11, 1927

I am writing this down to make an accurate record of what happened to me last night at Sarbe Springs. I either saw and felt a haint, or had a nightmare while I was wide awake.

On October 10, 1927, I was in my right mind, cold sober, and a-mind to go courting Lillie. After supper, I saddled old Whiteface and rode down to the DeHart farm. It was still light when I got there, so we walked through the punkin patch down by the creek. When we got out of sight, I kissed her and we both felt happy.

I'd been thinking about popping the question, and I did. She said yes, but I had to ask her pa. It was getting dark when we got back to the house. Her pa and ma were sitting in rocking chairs on the porch. I just blurted it out and he said okay to get married when I got a place to take her. We talked a heap longer than I wanted to, but it had to be.

It was close to midnight when I took my leave to come home. The moon was full, and I felt happiness running from the top of my head to the tip of my toes. Whiteface knew the way home, so I just sat in the saddle and thought about what a wedding night with Lillie would be like.

With no warning, Whiteface bolted and paid no heed to my frantic pulls on the reigns. In a flash of cold terror, I realized we were passing Sarbe Springs. I caught a glimpse of a figure jumping at me from the bank.

The next instant, I felt a death grip around my waist. I had to hang on to the reigns with both hands, so I could not wrestle with whoever, or whatever, had hold of me. I have never been so terrified in my life. The grip was cold, then hot, and I could feel something leaning against my back.

When Whiteface galloped past the road to the house, the grip on me left, and Whiteface stopped dead in his tracks. He needed to rest and I needed to get my wits back. I looked up at the full moon and asked for help. I've never gone to the altar and been saved so I didn't know how to pray.

I'd had to admit to Lillie's ma and pa that I had not been saved, but tried to live right. Her ma had urged me to "get right" with God, but her pa didn't say anything, because he is what they call a backslider.

After a while, Whiteface cooled down and I got calm. I gave him a nudge and he trotted back to the road to our house, and went to the barn. I stayed in the barn with him and thought about what had happened at Sarbe Springs.

I've always laughed at everybody who tells tales about haints jumping off the bank at Sarbe Springs onto their horses, or walking along with them, but I won't any more. I have rode past there hundreds of times, and this is the first time I ever saw and felt anything I can't explain.

This time I saw and felt a "thing." But I don't know what it was. Whatever it was, it scared the hell out me. And, one thing is for damn certain, Whiteface and I did not imagine that "thing" at the same time.

I now believe that the haints out there can scare people to death, but I have not heard tell of anybody being hurt. Lillie always says she sees a woman walking when we go by there, night or day. She swears to me it's a woman who lost her love in the Civil War.

I don't want to make Lillie afraid. She don't seem to be scared when she sees them. After I marry Lillie, I may tell her and I may not, because in the light of day I feel like a fool.

/s/ Oliver Shepherd

Oliver married Lillie, but he never told her what happened at Sarbe Springs the night she promised to marry him, nor about other encounters with haints. In later accounts, he called them ghosts. After he died at 56, Lillie found detailed accounts among his papers, and thankfully, they were preserved by my pack-rat aunt.

### What People Living Today Say

During the past two years, I have talked with many cousins and residents of the Alarka community about the tales of the Sarbe Springs Haints/Ghosts. Most dismiss the idea as nonsense, others believe the tales, and two swear they have encountered them personally.

My first cousin, Dearl Shepherd Crisp, grew up in the Alarka Community. She knew all about Oliver Shepherd's experience since her father was his great-uncle.

When I went to visit Dearl to talk about the Sarbe Spring haints, she reminded me that several years ago, she had talked with me and my husband, Jesse, about them and that I had not taken any of the tales seriously.

She recalled my attitude correctly, because at the time we were seeking information about a lone grave we had come upon while looking at some acreage, that joins the property where Sarbe Springs is located, that we were considering buying for a tree farm.

The grave was well kept, but the headstone inscription had weathered so severely it could not be read.

Dearl told us that the person buried there was a woman who lived all of her life in the Alarka community, and in her later life everyone called her "Aunt Patty Brendle."

She had a child out of wedlock by David Shepherd, a relative of ours, but I did not fathom his exact location in our family tree. He built a small log cabin on a parcel of his property for Aunt Patty and the child. The child died quite young, but she lived there until she died during the flu epidemic about 1918.

Aunt Parry never forgave Shepherd for "not making her an honest woman." And so, Dearl says, a lot of people think the haint that looks like a woman is Aunt Patty.

Dearl has replaced the headstone, and built a fence to guard the grave from encroachment, or obliteration, by the present property owners.

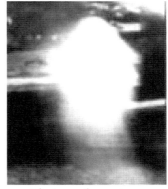

Photograph courtesy Rose Collier

After our first conversation with Dearl about the grave marker, Jesse and I contracted to buy the property. The owner could not make us a clear title, so we got our money back.

This may account for the problems Dearl is experiencing with the present property owners getting too close to Aunt Patty's grave. I suggested to Dearl that she enlist Aunt Patty's help. If she "appeared" and told them where the property lines are, that would probably be effective!

### Jacob Baines Took to the Creek

I heard a story about Jacob Baines from several people. There were minor variances in some of the details, but the major elements in the story were consistent. What follows is my summary of it.

Jacob Baines, whom everybody called "Old Jake," lived on what residents refer to as "the head of Alarka," for about 60 years. He was born there and died there about 1940. The "head of Alarka" at that time was at the place where Alarka road ended. Beyond his house were the wilds of the Alarka Mountains. Alarka Road ran from State Highway 19 to his house.

For many years, about once a month, Old Jake drove a wagon, pulled by a team of two mules, from the head of Alarka to Bryson City, the nearest town. He hauled produce, moonshine, and good kindling wood to town, and brought back supplies and money. He did not trust banks.

Everybody knew Old Jake's route to and from town. He always took a detour from Alarka Road down to a shallow spot in Alarka Creek and drove across to the other side. He drove on that road for a couple of miles, then crossed back over the creek to Alarka Road.

No one had observed that his route was a detour around Sarbe Springs until a school teacher who had just arrived in

Swain County to teach at the Alarka School, asked him about it. Without hesitation, Old Jake told him why and gave him a neighborly warning.

Old Jake said that long years before he'd lost one mule after he rounded the curve at Sarbe Springs and saw a *headless horseman* coming at him. He vowed he could see it was a *headless horseman* because the sun was just going down. The mules bolted so hard that he lost control of them, and the wagon crashed down the bank below the road.

He said he was scared to death but got out with a couple of broken fingers, and bruises that took months to heal. One mule survived but he had to shoot the other one because it broke two legs. He swore that day never to drive his wagon near Sarbe Springs again.

Old Jake said he'd heard about the headless horseman before he saw it but did not believe in it. He does not have a theory on "who" it might be, but knew what he had to do. "I don't really give a damn who he is, I ain't going to tangle with him again! If the creek's too high, I just wait it out."

### An Anti-Ghost Chant

A friend offered advice on how to keep a haint/ghost from following me home, and I'll share it with you!

When you get to your door, stop and spin counter clockwise three times, real fast, and chant in a loud voice:

Ghosts and spirits — Turn! Spin!
Get dizzy in the head!

Go back where you belong —
Cause you're dead!

## Chapter 14
## Do Angels Sing on Roan Mountain?

**Question:** Do angels sing on Roan Mountain?
**Answer:** Many ear witnesses say they do.

**Question:** Is there music on Roan Mountain?
**Answer:** Many ear witnesses say yes.

**Question:** Is there always sound on Roan Mountain?
**Answer:** All ear witnesses say yes.

No doubt about it, sounds and intrigue go hand in hand on Roan Mountain! This has spawned delightful stories, myths, legends and mysteries. We'll take a look at Roan Mountain and some of them.

### Roan Mountain

Roan Mountain is on the boundary between Tennessee and North Carolina, and is part of Pisgah and Cherokee national forests. Its five-mile-long ridge rises to 6,285 feet. The Appalachian Trail crosses it. The nearest towns are Bakersville, North Carolina, and Roan Mountain, Tennessee.

Fittingly, for this cauldron of the unexplained, the origin of the name *Roan* for this mountain has been lost. There are many legends about the name, and here are three of them.

■ Legend — It is named for Daniel Boone's roan horse. Daniel Boone was one of the frontier settlers who ignored the British ban of 1763 against travel in the Appalachian Mountains. On one trip through the area, his horse became lame and Boone left him in a valley next to a creek.

The next year he was traveling through the same area, and surprised he find his roan horse — fat and healthy.

Boone reclaimed his horse, and began to call the creek where he had left his horse as Roan Creek, and the valley Roan Valley. Eventually the name was officially adopted for the mountain that rises from Roan Valley.

■ Legend — Roan Mountain is named for the berries on the mountain ash trees that grow on the mountain. The berries grow in big clusters. The green berries turn to "roan"

color, and in September to scarlet. And, of course, there are facts and legends to go with the beauty!

Mountain ash is also known as the Rowan tree It is important to know about the Rowan tree because, according to folklore, it has magical powers. Rowan wood is potent against bad luck or evil. No witch can enter a house with a Rowan tree growing in its yard.

Walking sticks are made of this wood for safe night journeys, and branches are often used as dowsing rods. Carrying a piece of Rowan wood will increase one's psychic powers.

And this magical tree warns when a severe winter is coming! The more berries on the tree, the more severe the winter will be. This came about in the long-ago time. The Great Spirit promised the Indians that whenever He was going to send a cold winter, He would cover the tree with food!

■ Legend — Roan Mountain gets its name from the crimson/dark magenta color rhododendrons that grow on it.

This legend is in the book, *Adventures in the wilds of the United States and British American provinces*, by Charles Lanman, published in 1856.

Photo courtesy Martin LaBar

"There was once a time when all the nations of the earth were at war with the Catawbas, and had proclaimed their determination to conquer and possess their country. On hearing this intelligence the Catawbas became greatly enraged, and sent a challenge to all their enemies, and dared them to a fight on the summit of the Roan.

"The challenge was accepted, and no less than three famous battles were fought. The streams of the entire land were red with blood, a number of tribes became extinct, and the Catawbas carried the day.

"Whereupon it was that the Great Spirit caused the forests to wither from the three peaks of the Roan Mountain where the battles were fought; and wherefore it is that the flowers which grow upon this mountain are chiefly of a crimson hue, for they are nourished by the blood of the slain."

### Legends About the "Mountain Music" on Roan Mountain

All ear witnesses agree that there are always sounds on Roan Mountain.

The sounds have been most described as:

- music
- wind
- singing
- bees buzzing
- snapping, sizzling, crackling, rustling, and smooth

Collectively, for convenience in communication, the sounds are called "mountain music."

### Do Ear Witnesses Hear Different Sounds?

Since Roan Mountain is actually not one mountain, but a high ridge about five miles long, do different witnesses hear different things because they are at different points? Possibly. But ear witnesses standing side by side report hearing different sounds!

Human beings interpret what they hear based on their perception of reality at the moment sound waves reach the brain. And the human auditory perception of what sounds are "music" and what sounds are "noise" differs from culture to culture, and generation to generation.

### Do Some Ear Witnesses Hear Angel Singing?

One of the most charming legends declares that a choir of angels hovers over Roan Mountain to practice the songs they will sing on Judgment Day.

On that fateful day the Lord God Almighty will open the record book, and each human being would be judged on the deeds done while living on Earth, and sent to Heaven or Hell.

The ear witnesses report that the powerful "hallelujahs" they heard cannot be produced with weak human vocal cords.

William Tillman, who has lived near Roan Mountain all his life, told me that he has heard its mountain music most of his life. His parents believed that God sent the Angel Choir to warn people about the "wages" of sin.

He believed it for a long time, and the sounds struck fear in his heart. But as the years went by the fear gradually faded, and he now thinks the mountain music is simply natural sounds.

Mr. Tillman remembers hearing the Angel Choir story in church services when he was young. The service closed with the congregation singing the hymn *A Beautiful Life*, with emphasis on the lines:

- "Life's Evening Sun is Sinking Low,
- A few more days and I must go.
- To meet the deeds that I have done,
- Where there will be no setting sun."

### Devil's Wind

Some people who have been eye witnesses as well as ear witnesses deduct that the Devil sends an evil wind to Roan Mountain to show his power.

When the evil wind comes, it herds the clouds into a perfect circle around the top of the mountain. They believe that the sound they hear while the wind is herding the clouds is the Devil singing a mournful song from hell.

There is always wind on Roan Mountain, from a gentle breeze undulating the long grass on the balds to killer velocities. The highest wind speed ever recorded in the area was on April 18, 1997, at the

weather station on nearby Grandfather Mountain — 195 miles per hour. The winds can sprinkle you with a soft and gentle rain, or they can usher in a deadly thunderstorm.

In 1799, John Strother, working with a surveyor on Roan Mountain, wrote that the wind was so powerful that it "blowed holes all over the northwest side of the mountain."

### Ear and Eye Witness — Pere Libourel

In 1888 Pere Libourel was a guest at the Cloudland Hotel on Roan Mountain. The hotel had been build in 1878 by Civil War hero General John Thomas Wilder, and attracted visitors from all over the world.

The mysterious "mountain music" was an amusing topic of conversation among the guests. Pere Libourel, a determined young man, told Wilder that he believed it was the Devil's wind that kept the top of Roan Mountain bald, and he was going up on the mountain to solve the mystery.

Wilder warned Libourel of the dangers he would face, and urged him not to go alone. The warnings fell on deaf ears He set out one cool morning with no food, water, or jacket.

Late that afternoon Libourel returned to the hotel, and without speaking a word, grabbed his bags and left. It was years before he told what he had seen on Roan Mountain.

When he finally told what had happened to him, he said that he was caught in a vicious thunderstorm, and thrown into a dark crevice, or cave, in the side of the mountain. There he came face-to-face with the source of the mountain music.

He saw a ghostly choir and heard them sing. The members of this choir were not, as some local people had told him, a choir of angels, but the souls of the damned writhing in hell.

After the music ceased, he crawled out of the dark place to flee. He gazed up at the clear blue sky, and saw what he described as a miracle. A dazzling rainbow had completely encircled the top of Roan Mountain!

He did not know it at the time, but Pere Libourel had seen a rainbow that people call "God's Halo."

### The Legend of God's Halo

There is a legend that after the fury of valley thunderstorms passes, and the mountain music ceases, a rainbow forms in a complete circle on top of the Roan. This rainbow is God's halo left to protect the Roan, and its visitors, from all that is evil.

I am indebted to Jennifer Bauer Laughlin, for granting me permission to include this account of her experience with a rainbow on Roan Mountain. She is a ranger naturalist at Roan Mountain State Park, and author of the book *Roan Mountain: A Passage of Time*, which is a delightful, comprehensive read about this legendary mountain.

■ One blustery day Jennifer Laughlin was to lead about fifty people on a full-moon hike to the highlands of the Roan. The weather was so threatening that she and a friend drove up the foggy mountainside to check the conditions. Just as they were about to turn back, the fog and clouds dropped away! They were under clear blue skies and could see the storms rolling in the valleys below. Here is what happened next, in her own words.

"I saw the most unbelievable phenomenon I have ever witnessed. A rainbow began to materialize at eyelevel, and as it developed it took the form of a complete circle. And then a second rainbow formed within the circle of the first!

"I can't say how long we stood there. It seemed like a short eternity before the elusive rainbow faded from view. I reaffirmed my faith in legends on the spot."

## What Scientist Say About Rainbows

Scientists now know that all rainbows are circular and form as a colored ring of light opposite the sun. In most geographical locations, the bottom part of the ring is blocked by the horizon, and only an arc of the rainbow can be seen.

Jennifer Laughlin and those who have been fortunate enough to be on top of the Roan when rainbows were formed were able to view the rainbow as a whole circle. Whole circles of rainbows can be see from airplanes and from space.

## Amy Pepperhill, Ear Witness

I met Amy Pepperhill at a writers' meeting. She is an avid hiker with a keen interest in mysteries. When she learned I was researching the sounds on Roan Mountain, she shared her experience with me, and gave me permission to write her story and print her poem "Metatron on Roan."

In October 1999 she and a friend were hiking on the Appalachian Trail, and decided to tackle Big Hump Bald in the Roan Highlands. Shortly after noon on the day they were hiking it, the temperature was 38 degrees, and the wind was about 30 miles per hour. This made for very uncomfortable conditions, but not rough enough to be life threatening.

They heard an eerie, somber sound. Amy said they joked about it and wanted to believe it was the wind whipping about in the grass and rocks. But the eerie sound seemed to be playing familiar tunes. It was constant and piercing. Neither of them could discern if the sound was from the natural element, an animal, human, or a musical instrument.

They felt embarrassed to admit their sense of unease, but the sound was constant and became stressful. They took a detour onto a country road to get away from the eerie sound. A weatherworn man was baling hay.

They introduced themselves and asked him if he had ever heard the mountain music. He told them he'd heard it all his life, and thought it was God's way of reminding people they don't know everything. He said his great-grandfather used to own a lot of land, including Big Hump Bald, but when they started to tax land he sold it for a pair of horseshoes.

After she returned safely from the hike, Amy penned a poem about her experience with the eerie sound, and it is printed here with her permission.

Before you read the poem, I am including a short explanation for the benefit of any reader who may not recognize the name Metatron, as I did not when I first heard the poem.

According to *A Dictionary of Angels*, Metatron is a biggie, the angel who sits on a throne next to The Throne, the very viceroy of the angels, whose specific job is to sustain mankind. Metatron has other names in the references I checked about angels, but Amy preferred Metatron because of its modern, technological ring.

**Metatron on Roan**
**by Amy Pepperhill**

High on the mountain they call Roan,
    Metatron hides an earthly throne.
Across Roan's ridge, that spans five miles,
    good and evil spirits all run wild.
When choirs of angels hover to sing,
    the Devil gets mad, and his wind brings.
We hear angels battle with all their might,
    and up on Roan it's a frightful sight.
But when it's time, God says, "Go!"
    and crowns the Roan with His Halo.

## Roan Mountain State Park

Roan Mountain State Park is part of the Tennessee State Parks system, about 16 miles south of Elizabethton, Tennessee.

A Rhododendron Festival is held there, at the foot of Roan Mountain, the third or fourth weekend in June, depending on the peak of the rhododendron bloom.

Detailed directions and information is available at:

- http://www.roanmountain.com/statepark.htm
- telephone1-800-250-8620.

## What Hikers Told Me About Roan Mountain

Roan Mountain is not for the lone novice, or faint of heart hikers. A harsh taskmaster lurks beneath its beauty.

View Roan Mountain, Tennessee Summit
Photograph courtesy Mike Calabrese, mikecalabrese@milecalabrese.com

## Chapter 15
## Mysterious Mounds

When explorers and settlers pushed into the valleys of Appalachia, they found earthen mounds.

To this day, the mounds have guarded the secret of who built them, or why.

Photograph courtesy Patricia C. Baker

This is Nikwasi Mound. It is on Business Route 441 close to the Tennessee River, in Franklin, North Carolina. It is owned by the Town of Franklin, and can be visited free of charge, thanks to many energetic citizens of Macon County who were determined to keep Nikwasi as a monument to history.

Casual passersby will probably glance at the mound and see it as a low hill. When explorers and settlers arrived, many of the mounds were overgrown with trees so that their outlines could barely be distinguished, although, once cleared, the mounds revealed their artificial nature by their regularity and symmetry of shape. Many of the mounds were cleared and utilized by the Cherokee in a variety of ways.

The newcomers assumed that the Cherokee people had built the mounds, but the tribal leaders declared that the mounds were in place when they came to the land, and disclaimed all knowledge of their origin, as well as the purposes for which they were erected. They acknowledged that they had built villages on the mounds, and had changed the size and shape of some of them to accommodate their needs, and lit sacred fires in them.

Most experts now agree that the mounds were erected by people who occupied the land, but vanished before the Cherokees arrived in the Smokies. Mounds in Western North Carolina and Tennessee date back to A.D. 1000-1500, and beyond.

Whoever erected the mounds worked with incredible persistence. Some covered several acres, and rose as high as 70 feet, while others were mere blisters. Since no sophisticated tools have been found, it is assumed that the dirt and mud had to be moved in baskets. Unearthed mounds have revealed layers added at different times. The mounds were used again and again by different people because of the long, hard work needed to build and maintain them.

The settlers who had claimed the fertile bottomlands to farm generally considered the mounds nuisances to be plowed flat as quickly as possible. Nikwasi almost suffered this fate.

### Nikwasi Was a Sacred Town

The Cherokee named the mound that is now in downtown Franklin "Nikwasi," and built a council house on it, and a village around it. There is no record of when the building was done but the village was inhabited in 1819 when North Carolina acquired it by treaty. The Cherokee were forced to move away, and the new residents named the village Franklin.

The council house was the tribe's religious center, and a sacred fire burned constantly on a raised altar, and sacred items were displayed there. It was also used for tribal councils, ceremonies, and social gatherings.

The Cherokees revered Nikwasi as a sacred town, and treasured myths about it. Perhaps the best loved-myth was recorded on pages 336-337 by James Mooney in his book *Myths of the Cherokees,* published in 1900, about a battle to save it.

The Cherokees believed that Nunnehi were a race of spirit people. They were "people who live anywhere," and were invisible except when they wanted to be seen, and then they looked and spoke just like other Indians.

### The Spirit Defender of Nikwasi

"Long ago a powerful unknown tribe invaded the country from the southeast, killing people and destroying settlements wherever they went. No leader could stand against them, and in a little while they had wasted all of the lower settlements and advanced into the mountains.

"The warriors of the old town of Nikwasi, on the head of Little Tennessee, gathered their wives and children into the townhouse and kept scouts constantly on the lookout for the presence of danger.

"One morning just before daybreak the spies saw the enemy approaching and at once gave the alarm. The Nikwasi men seized their arms and rushed out to meet the attack, but after a long, hard fight they found themselves overpowered and began to retreat. Suddenly a stranger stood among them and shouted to the chief to call off his men and he himself would drive back the enemy.

"From the dress and language of the stranger, the Nikwasi people thought him a chief who had come with reinforcements from the Overhill settlements in Tennessee. They fell back along the trail, and as they came near the townhouse they saw a great company of warriors coming out from the side of the mound as through an open doorway.

"Then they knew that their friends were the Nunnehi, the Immortals, although no one had ever heard before that they lived under the Nikwasi mound.

"The Nunnehi poured out by hundreds, armed and painted for the fight, and the most curious thing about it all was that they became invisible as soon as they were fairly outside of the settlement, so that although the enemy saw the glancing arrow or the rushing tomahawk, and felt the stroke, he could not see who sent it.

"Before such invisible foes the invader soon had to retreat. They tried to shield themselves behind rocks and trees, but the Nunnehi arrows went around the rocks and killed them from the other side, and they could find no hiding place. When not more than a dozen were left alive, they cried out for mercy."

### Nikwasi is Saved!

The Nunnehi chief told them they had deserved their punishment for attacking a peaceful tribe, and he spared their lives and told them to go home and take the news to their people. This was the Indian custom — always to spare a few to carry back the news of the defeat.

The enemy went away, and the Nunnehi went back to the mound. And they are still there, because during the Civil War when a strong party of Union troops came to surprise a handful of Confederates, they saw so many soldiers guarding the town of Franklin that they were afraid, and went away without making an attack.

In 2002, Nikwasi is guarded externally. And one wonders whether the Nunnehi are not on guard internally! Listen — are drumbeats mingling with the traffic noises?

### A Flesh-and-Blood Defender of Nikwasi

Nikwasi was saved from being plowed flat on one occasion by Gilmer Andrew Jones, a prominent Franklin attorney.

When Jones was a child, he lived near an Indian family and learned something of the Cherokee culture and their language. In his later years, he was a voluntary legal advisor to the Eastern Band of Cherokees and took part in tribal councils held at Oconoluftee.

The story quoted here is reported by Barbara McRae in her book *Franklin's Ancient Mound.*

"The extent to which Jones would go in preserving the monument (Nikwasi) was illustrated by an incident in the mid-1930s, when he spotted Harold Sloan plowing corn with a mule on the south side of the mound.

"Jones tried to dissuade Sloan from plowing too close and causing erosion. As the argument escalated, the mule trotted off, pulling the plow behind. The two men gave chase and finally caught the animal after several trips around the mound.

"They were, of course, observed, and the incident became famous in the family as the 'Sloan-Jones Oratorical Meeting,' moderated by a jackass."

### Saved Again!

In 1946, W. Roy Carpenter, the owner of Nikwasi, proposed to level it for a commercial lot. Jones and others founded the Macon County Historical Society and launched a successful campaign, and were able to purchase it several years later.

It was conveyed to the Town of Franklin as trustee for the residents of Macon County, with the stipulation that the mound be preserved, just as it stands, for the residents of Macon and for posterity, and that it not to be used for any commercial purpose.

### Kituwah Mound

Kituwah is believed to be the first permanent settlement of the ancient Cherokee, and is revered as a sacred place. It is located beside the Tuckaseigee River, on State Highway 19, in Swain County, North Carolina, between Cherokee and Bryson City. How high it might have been at its zenith, no one has determined precisely.

According to legend and belief, this is the place where religious leaders shared divinely ordained laws and ethical codes after receiving them from spirits on Clingmans Dome, and the Cherokee became the "Ani-Kitu'hwagi," the Principal People, a name still used by many Cherokee.

Photograph courtesy Patricia C. Baker

There is archaeological evidence of near-continuous occupation for 10,000 years. In the summer of 2001, an 8,000-year-old soapstone bowl was found.

The Cherokee lost Kituwah in 1821, and the sacred fire within the great mound was extinguished. Chief Yonaguska was evicted by the county sheriff because the state of North Carolina did not honor the federal deed to the property. It was seized and sold at a state auction in Waynesville.

The Kituwah property was sold many more times, and it is known to have been used as a dairy farm, tomato field and packing place, a cornfield, and even a grass airstrip, Ferguson Field.

Many Cherokees kept their faith that the sacred fire smoldered within Kituwah and that one day it would be returned to them. There are many stories in their oral tradition about strange sightings of smoke rising from the mound and the sound of drumbeats during the Civil War.

But now Kituwah is back in the hands of the Cherokee. In 1996, the Eastern Band of Cherokee Indians paid more than $3 million for a 309-acre tract that includes the mound and the sacred village.

The Band will make a decision on whether to preserve Kituwah or take advantage of the site's economic possibilities. The decision will decide the fate of the richest, most significant archaeological Indian site in western North Carolina. In addition to a treasure trove of artifacts, Kituwah contains remains from countless human burials.

### Mounds Contain Records of Daily Life and Death

Since council houses were built on the mounds, scientists have ascertained that a series of successive council houses are buried within some of them.

Walls, central hearths and entryways have been uncovered in some mounds. These same items have been documented by the use of gradiometers without disturbing the mound.

Pottery used for cooking and storing food has been found in excavated mounds. Some of the pottery styles are complex and varied, with elaborate stamped and incised designs. Religious relics, tools, and large capped pots, used as burial urns for infants or to hold the cremated remains of adults, have been uncovered.

Human remains have been found in the mounds by people tilling the land, and while many were left in place, others were destroyed. Since 1968, when the American Indian Movement was formed, a vigorous campaign has been conducted to halt any digging of Native American bones, and to preserve those known to exist.

In various ways, many of the remains are now at the University of North Carolina at Chapel Hill. The National Park Service, in accordance with the Native American Graves Protection and Repatriation Act (NAGPRA), posted a notice in the Federal Register on August 9, 1999 (Volume 64, Number 152, Pages 43222-43223), that an inventory of the remains at Chapel Hill had been completed.

## Other Mounds

Known and unknown mound builders inhabited many parts of the United States. They built mounds unique to their part of the country, and are wonderful sites to visit.

The Etowah Indian Mounds State Park in Cartersville, Georgia, preserves 7 mounds, portions of the original village that was once on the site, and a museum. Park information is available at:
- http://ngeorgia.com/parks/etowah.html
- Phone: 770 387-3747.

*Thank you for being here.*

*I wish you robust health and happy reading.*

*http://www.juanittabaldwin.com*